THE CHAMPAK STORY BOX

RUPA

Published by
Rupa Publications India Pvt. Ltd 2022
7/16, Ansari Road, Daryaganj
New Delhi 110002

Sales Centres:
Allahabad Bengaluru Chennai
Hyderabad Jaipur Kathmandu
Kolkata Mumbai

ISBN: 978-93-5520-396-0

First impression 2022

10 9 8 7 6 5 4 3 2 1

Printed in India

TABLE OF CONTENTS

 SCIENCE   ALIENS

 SLAPSTICK HUMOUR   SPACE

 FANTASY   TECHNOLOGY

MYSTERY

IT'S A RIOT

By S Varalakshmi

Two crocodiles named Crio and Wendy lived near Lake Caramel.

One day, when they were lying under the sun, Crio suggested, "Let us visit that restaurant on the other side of our lake. What do you say, Wendy?"

Wendy turned to look at the restaurant and joked, "Yeah, as though somebody has invited us for lunch!"

Frowning, Crio asked, "Why not?" Wendy explained patiently, "Because that restaurant is strictly for humans, and as far as I can see, we aren't."

Crio said, "Doesn't matter. That sign reads 'Everyone is Welcome!'."

Wendy knew from experience it was no use arguing with Crio, so she left it at that. But Crio kept urging her. "Come on, don't be a spoilsport. Let's go. It is not as if we have been to restaurants many times."

Wendy reluctantly agreed even though a warning bell rang in her head as it always did whenever she decided to go along with Crio's ideas. She knew from experience that an epic **DISASTER** was soon to follow!

THE CROCS EAT OUT

Both set out towards the restaurant, which looked pretty crowded.

They stood outside, behind a bush. They saw that the parking lot was packed with cars and were wondering how to get inside.

The **AROMA** of food from the restaurant made their tummies rumble with hunger.

Famished, they decided to make their entry.

As they pushed opened the glass door, all eyes fell on them.

The humans just stared in shock. Seeing the two crocodiles smiling at them resulted in **panic**, and very soon, high-pitched screams pierced the air.

People dropped their food and jostled against each other to get away.

Puzzled, Crio asked, "Wendy, why are they screaming?"

Wendy replied, "How do I know? Don't say I didn't warn you though."

Then, Crio looked around but didn't find anything that could have caused this COMMOTION.

Wendy caught sight of a man dangling from the ceiling while holding onto a **CHANDELIER**.

For some reason, he was staring at Wendy and screaming at the top of his voice. "Weird people!" Wendy thought.

Confused, they both stepped inside and made their way towards an empty table and sat down.

But the screams rose an **octave**. Crio and Wendy smiled and looked around **amiably**.

IT'S TIME FOR LUNCH

As they sat down, the diners dashed towards the entrance, elbowing each other in a mad rush to escape. Cars screeched and pulled away. Within seconds, there was complete silence everywhere.

Baffled, Crio asked, "What's with everyone?"

Wendy replied, "Who cares? We came here to eat. Now, where is the waiter?"

They waited for some time, but no one arrived.

Crio was getting **IMPATIENT**, so he told Wendy to remain seated while he checked in the kitchen, which was at the far end of the dining room.

In the kitchen, Crio found five very busy cooks. It looked as though they were unaware of what had happened in the dining room.

A preoccupied waiter carrying an order stopped short when he spotted Crio just a couple of feet in front of him.

At the sight of the huge crocodile smiling at him, he let out a terrified scream and dropped the **tray**.

Soon his screams were matched with those of the cooks who ran away through the back door.

Crio looked blank for a second and thought, "These humans are really weird. Always screaming at the drop of a hat!"

A DELICIOUS MEAL

Crio's mouth watered as he looked at the cooked **FOOD**, the aroma of which was tickling his nostrils and making his tummy growl in hunger.

He grabbed two large trays and filled them with four large pizzas, fries, pastries and ice-cream sodas.

He then carried them over to Wendy, who was waiting patiently for him.

"Where were you, Crio? What took you so long?" she asked.

Crio then narrated everything.

Wendy said, "Strange people. It doesn't matter. Let us have our lunch. I am famished. To kill time, I have been gulping down litres of water here," she grumbled, pointing to the jugs of water.

Crio and Wendy ate to their heart's content.

Smacking his lips, Crio said **ENTHUSIASTICALLY**, "This food is great, Wendy. Simply out of this world. Shall we come here again with our friends?"

Warming to the idea, Wendy replied, "Why not? The more, the merrier! We can even have a party here. And next time, let us hope the humans don't behave in this ridiculous manner."

~ ☀ ~

THAT'S NOT RIGHT

Some things in this picture are not right. Find out what they are.

GHOSTS ON THE BANYAN TREE

By Hema Madan

As Chika the Rabbit walked back to her house, her **HEARTBEAT** sped up.

It had turned dark, and she was afraid of the dark.

She always made sure to avoid going anywhere after dark, but today while she was **PLAYING** with her friends she had not realised how late it was. The strange noises around her were making her nervous.

She was closer to her house now, but she still had to walk past the big **BANYAN** tree.

Chika was scared to walk past the big banyan tree, as she had heard many scary stories about it from her friends.

It was known to be a home for **GHOSTS**. Her friend Manny the Mongoose had once told her a story of his **encounter** with a ghost. He had to run for his life after the shadows had tried to catch hold of him.

As she walked further and got closer to the tree, Chika started to feel nervous. She had never been there alone after dark since she had found out it was haunted.

The wind had also started to blow, and the sound of the rustling leaves was making things worse for her.

She jumped as she heard the sound of a branch cracking. Her mobile battery had died too, and there was no way she could call anybody to escort her home.

She started walking faster, as it had started to get cold. She could hear strange whispering noises now. She started to run, but she was stopped in her tracks by the shadows in front of her.

She froze with fear, and her feet wouldn't move. Tears started to roll down her cheeks, and she could hear her heart pounding.

CHIKA MEETS A GHOST

Suddenly, she felt something land on her head with a slight thump. She screamed and started to run faster. She could feel the strange thing CRAWL down her back. Chika ran as fast as she could. The laughter that followed **scared** her to her bone.

She stopped only when she saw Jumbo the Elephant standing in front of her house.

Jumbo was Chika's neighbour and FRIEND who always looked out for her. Jumbo had seen her running and the fear on her face troubled him.

He asked Chika with concern, "What is it, Chika? You look pale and FRIGHTENED! Is everything okay?"

"No, I am not okay, Jumbo. Ghosts were chasing me, and one even tried to sit on my head. I am lucky I could get away from them," replied Chika.

"Don't tell me you believe in those ghost stories floating around, Chika. Superstitious people made them up," said Jumbo.

"No, Jumbo. I saw shadows with my own eyes, and I heard WHISPERS. Those stories are all true," Chika argued.

JUMBO STRIVES TO RESOLVE THE SITUATION

"Chika take me to where you saw the ghosts and show me what you saw. I want to take this fear out of your mind once and for all," Jumbo suggested.

"There's no way I am going back there again at this time," Chika refused.

"Chika, I have always looked after you, and I want you to TRUST me and take me there," insisted Jumbo.

Chika finally agreed to take Jumbo to the big banyan tree. Soon they reached it, and Chika could again hear the whispers. She hid behind Jumbo and pointed at the SHADOWS, which Jumbo saw and laughed. Chika was surprised and asked, "Why are you laughing, Jumbo? Aren't you scared?"

Jumbo smiled and said, "Just wait here; let me show you something." He went near the tree and pulled out a long piece of cloth from one of the branches with his TRUNK. He called Chika and showed it to her. "You see, Chika? It is nothing but the shadow of this cloth that you saw. It was stuck to a branch and was flying in the breeze," Jumbo said.

"But what about the whispers?" Chika asked.

"A family of **lizards** live on this tree, and the noise is their murmurs," said Jumbo.

"I fell on you earlier, and we all had a good laugh as you ran with fear," a tiny lizard said as he came down the tree.

"Oh! That explains the laughter I heard," said Chika.

Jumbo laughed too and said, "Yes, Chika. I am happy that I could show you the truth. Now you can do the same for your friends."

The lizard family joined them as they laughed.

~ ☀ ~

MONSTER COOKIES

You need:

- 1 cup whole wheat flour, sifted
- ½ cup oats
- ½ cup finely ground almonds
- ¾ tsp baking powder
- ¼ tsp baking soda
- 1 ½ cup jaggery
- ½ cup butter
- 1 tsp cinnamon
- 1 tbsp chia seeds soaked in 4 tbsp warm water for 10 minutes
- Milk, if required

Adult: Pre-heat the oven to 175°C. Line a baking tray with parchment paper.

How to make:

1. Whisk the butter and jaggery together in a bowl until mixed properly.
2. Add all the dry ingredients to it and mix it gently with a spatula.
3. If the dough mixture is crumbly, add 1 tablespoon of milk at a time till it becomes smooth.
4. Divide the dough into 12 to 14 equal parts. Roll it into balls, flatten it and put it on a tray.
5. Add gems, edible sugar eyes, and nuts to decorate the cookies.
6. Bake for 15 to 20 minutes until the cookies are golden brown. Take them out of the oven.
7. Add gummy sweets carefully before the cookies cool.
8. Enjoy the monster cookies!

BHINDI BRAWL

By Muraly TV

"Smash his house!" screamed Farhan the Fox.

"Thrash him to a pulp!" shouted Wally the Wolf. An aggrieved **CROWD** had gathered in front of Dodo the Donkey's house.

"What's wrong with Dodo?" asked Tahir the Tiger curiously.

"Dodo was making **FOOLS** of us by pretending to be our well-wisher," Farhan said. "It has been a month since he started residing in our Anandvan. We never checked his credentials."

"Before we pay the price for our innocence, we must teach him a lesson and throw him out of Anandvan," Wally growled.

"Dodo is nice; I don't think he would harm us," intervened Sapna the Squirrel.

A CRIMINAL IN THEIR MIDST

"Listen to this first and then comment," Wally said and played an audio clip on his phone.

"I love the taste of ladies' fingers. Today, I cut a few and tasted them. Wow! So dElicioUs!" Everyone heard the audio in shock. "I am planning to cut more ladies' fingers in the coming days before they lose their tenderness."

"It is Dodo's voice," Tahir confirmed.

"We must make our people aware of the health benefits of eating ladies' fingers," said a sweet female voice in the audio.

"Oh, Dodo and a woman are involved in this," Sapna concluded.

"It seems, Dodo belongs to some international gang." Coco the Cuckoo said, "We ladies are in danger now."

"Don't worry, we are here to PROTECT our ladies," Monu the Monkey said sternly.

Sensing something wrong, Dodo opened his windows. "Good morning, ladies and—"

Before Dodo could complete his sentence, Farhan screamed, "How dare you?"

"We may be uneducated, but we're not cowards. We are here to protect our ladies," Wally shouted.

"Before he escapes, let's break his house and catch him," Eddy the Elephant trumpeted. The animals surrounded Dodo's house, blocking all its exit doors.

CLEARING THE ANIMAL'S MISCONCEPTION

"Stop! Stop!" Pihu the Parrot said as she appeared from nowhere. "Aren't you ashamed of attacking—"

Before Pihu could finish speaking, Coco screamed, "Wally, please play the audio once again. I think the lady in the audio is Pihu."

"We must make our people aware of the health benefits of eating ladies' fingers." Once again, everybody heard the sweet voice and were shocked.

"Yes, it's my voice," Pihu said.

"What? You belong to the **notorious** gang too?" Coco wondered.

Meanwhile, Dodo came out of his house with a big sack on his back, holding a knife.

"Pihu, let's chop the ladies' fingers into different shapes and prepare various dishes."

Coco, Sapna, Sweety, Lovely, Monu and the other ladies screamed in fear when Dodo said it openly. They hid behind Eddy. Everyone was in shock.

"Oh! I just realised what happened," Pihu said and started laughing, while the others stared at them in fear.

Dodo and Pihu opened the sack, "Here are the ladies' fingers that we had cut yesterday."

"OOOOOHHHHHHH!" everybody screamed; a few closed their eyes.

"Don't try to fool us by showing us *bhindi*. Bring the ladies' fingers and surrender," Wally shouted at Dodo.

Before the situation could take an ugly turn, Pihu said, "I think, Farhan and Wally overheard Dodo's discussion with me last night, right?"

Farhan and Wally nodded hesitatingly. "There is nothing to worry about," Pihu said. "Farhan and Wally misunderstood our discussion. We were talking about our business of selling *bhindi*. The English name for *bhindi* is ladies' fingers."

Everybody burst into laughter. Dodo gifted the *bhindi* to everyone. "Now, let's taste *bhindi* masala, *bhindi* fry, *bhindi* sambar, *bhindi* dahi and have some fun," Pihu said as she served everyone.

THE BENEFITS OF *BHINDI*

"I like to see *bhindi* on plants, but I really don't like to eat them," Piggy the Piglet admitted.

"If you start eating *bhindi*, then you will be healthier," Pihu said.

"We eat so many leaves, fruits and vegetables. What's so special about *bhindi*?" asked Monu, who didn't like *bhindi* either. Patty the Puppy, Gigi the Giraffe and Katty the Kitten also had the same question in mind.

"Hmm...I think I will share the health benefits of eating *bhindi*," said Pihu.

"It's delicious, so that's the benefit of eating it," said Sapna.

"**Bhindi** is good for your eyes as it contains a good amount of **Carotenoids** that maintain vision," said Pihu.

"Carotenoids are required for the growth and repair of your skin cells. They also reduce the damage done to your skin by UV rays that come from the sun. So, if you eat sufficient *bhindi*, you will have healthy skin," Pihu explained.

"Right now, as we are facing the coronavirus pandemic, can *bhindi* help us in any way?" Gigi asked mischievously.

"Why not?" Dodo replied, "*Bhindi* has Vitamin C in abundance, which boosts **immunity**."

"Then, I will start eating lots of *bhindi* from today. I can then claim to be a coronavirus warrior," replied Gigi confidently. Everybody laughed. "Eating *bhindi* helps in weight loss, relieves constipation, lowers fat levels, reduces the risks of certain cancers and is even good for the heart," Dodo explained.

"*Bhindi* contains lots of calories, protein, carbohydrates, fat, folic acid, Vitamin C, Vitamin K, magnesium, fibre, calcium, potassium, iron and many more nutrients," said Pihu.

Everyone was excited to hear so many health benefits that can be obtained from one vegetable.

DIFFERENT WAYS TO ENJOY *BHINDI*

Dodo invited everybody to his *bhindi* farm. The **PALM** looked green and fresh. "*Bhindi* plants look so beautiful," said Sapna. "I love the flowers," Coco said.

"Can I eat the bigger ones?" asked Piggy. "It's better to eat the medium-sized ones that aren't too long because **BULGY** bhindis have very big seeds, which spoil the taste," said Pihu.

"Before eating, we have to cut off both its ends. Also, avoid using those with bruises and cuts. Always check for any worms or insects in it."

"*Krum, mrum, krum,*" Piggy munched on the *bhindi* with Monu, Gigi, Patty and Katty.

"We can prepare different dishes with *bhindi*. It can be cut in different shapes," said Pihu, who cut and showed them.

"It's sliced," screamed Sapna.

"It's now chopped," said Coco.

"Now, I am cutting it **DIAGONALLY**. We can even fry the whole *bhindi* till it's crunchy," Pihu explained.

"Hello, if anyone wants any help to cut ladies' fingers, just call me," Farhan said HUMOROUSLY out of the blue.

"And, to cook ladies' fingers, I will be there," Wally laughed.

And, no ladies tried to hide behind Eddy this time!

~ ~

SPACE WALK

By Vandana Gupta

One evening, eight-year-old Ria was watching a TV programme about how people worked in the international **space station**. Ria saw that people were floating. She was puzzled to see this. She asked, "Mother, why are astronauts FLOATING like this?

"Ria, our Earth has gravity that attracts everything to her. That's why we and other things can stand firm on land. There is no gravity in space, so everything floats there," explained Ma.

RIA WANTS TO SPACE-WALK

"No, I want to space-walk right now! Can't **gravity** disappear from the earth and we all float in the air?" asked Ria wistfully.

"No my child, it can't be so," Ma stated.

Ma tried to make Ria understand, but she was adamant about going to space now. Ma explained that people who go to space, undertake **rigorous** training and do lots of practice and only then are they able to function without gravity, but Ria wouldn't listen.

"Okay. When stars come out at night, I'll tell them to fulfil your wish," said Ma.

Ma thought that by night Ria would forget about the space-walk. But Ria was bent on freeing the earth of gravity and eagerly waited for the night so that her wish could come true.

A WISH COMES TRUE

At night, Ria told the **STARS** of her desire before going to bed.

When Ria woke up in the morning, she saw her bed floating in the air along with all the things in her room.

"My wish is fulfilled!" cried Ria with joy.

"Ria, quickly brush your teeth! You are getting late for school," mother shouted and Ria rushed inside the bathroom.

But she couldn't run, she was floating in the air. She was unable to remain on the floor. Somehow, she reached the bathroom. The bucket, mug, brush, toothpaste, soap— everything was flying in the air.

With great difficulty, Ria found and held her toothbrush. Then, she put toothpaste on the brush. After brushing her teeth, as she spat, the spit **scattered** in the air instead of in the basin.

"This means, if I spit, pee or poo, it will float in the air?" Ria was filled with disgust.

She tried to open the tap to rinse her mouth but water too, started floating in the air. With great difficulty, she held onto some drops of water, washed her mouth and came out of the bathroom floating.

"Ma, what have you prepared for tiffin today?" she asked floating to the kitchen.

"See what has happened here! The stove, utensils, boxes, vegetables, everything is floating in the air. I couldn't cook anything! Today take some fruits to school." Ria felt sad to hear that she wouldn't be able to eat Ma's delicious food.

TIME FOR SCHOOL

It also took a lot of time for Ria to get ready and pack her bag. She caught hold of the things floating in the air with difficulty. She put FRUITS in her lunch bag and floated towards her bus stop.

"Today I am late. I must have missed the bus!" she thought. But she was surprised to see the scene on the road. Her school bus was not there. It may have floated away somewhere.

All the children were floating in the air. Ria didn't even know the way to her school. She would normally sit in the bus and reach school.

Every student and teacher came in late, as everyone had the same problem as Ria. The scene in the CLASSROOM was spectacular! Desks, chairs, books—everything, was floating in the air.

"Where do I put my bag?" one child asked.

"Hold it in your hands or it will float; mine had floated," replied another.

"How will we write or take out our books and notebooks if we keep holding on to our bags and water bottles?" Akash cried.

Just then, their teacher came floating in and reached the blackboard with difficulty. Catching hold of the chalk in the air, she tried to write but couldn't do it properly.

"Ma'am, today teach us without writing," said Ria.

The period got over with the students and teacher trying to adjust to having 'no gravity'. Similar problems arose in all the other periods as well.

UNFORESEEN CONSEQUENCES

During the lunch break, Ria took out the fruits, but couldn't hold the apple properly. It floated away. But she somehow ate a guava.

"My mother couldn't cook food today, so I had to bring **fruits**," she said sadly.

"My mother also couldn't cook. I have brought **BISCUITS**," said Nitin.

"And I just have **BREAD**," cried Tiara.

During the games period, all the kids were hungry. "Today we will not play. I feel weak because I couldn't have breakfast," said Akash.

"We can't play even if we want to. When we throw the ball, it floats here and there," said Manisha, trying to play basketball.

"My shuttlecock is also straying. We can't play badminton also!" said Siddhu in distress.

Ria felt thirsty and opened her bottle. But the water went all around and Minu got wet. Similarly, Ria got wet when other children opened their water bottles. All the children's clothes and bags were **wet**.

School got over and the children started searching for their bags.

HEADING HOME

"Ria, have you seen my red bag anywhere? asked Nitin.

"Yes, look! It's flying near the window. Hold it quickly! If it flies out, you will never catch it," Minu replied. Nitin stuck his head out of the window, trying to hold his bag.

"Ria, have you got your bag," asked Minu. "No, I am looking for it," replied Ria.

Just then, Aarav shouted, "Ria! I saw your bag floating outside in the corridor." Ria dragged herself outside and got hurt when she knocked against the **WALL**.

Somehow, the children held onto their bags, hitting against each other or the tables, chairs and walls and floated towards their homes.

On the way home, some construction work was going on. Bricks and sand were floating in the air. Ria moved with great difficulty, saving her head from the BRICKS. Her eyes were half-closed to stop the sand from entering them and she took a wrong turn.

"Hey, Ria! Where are you going? Our home is this way," shouted Pankaj, Ria's friend who lived in her building.

"Pankaj, I can't control where I am going," cried Ria.

"But you will reach too far if you float away like this," Pankaj said.

"Then what should I do?"

"Hold on to something to stop. Then, move in the direction of your home," instructed Pankaj.

Just then, Ria saw a tree and held its branch. Ria was tired and hungry. She was unable to go home and was afraid she wouldn't be able to hold onto the branch for long. She held it tightly and cried, "I don't want space on Earth. Our earlier earth was better than this!"

ONLY A DREAM

"Hey, Ria! What's happened to you? Why are you holding my hand tightly and which Earth's better?" Ma asked while trying to wake Ria. Ria opened her eyes and saw that all the things in the room were in their place. She sighed in relief.

"Why are you so scared? Did you have a nightmare?" asked Ma lovingly.

"No Ma, it was a good dream," laughed Ria. "It made me realise, I want gravity on earth."

"Now get up and brush your teeth. You are late for school!" said Ma.

"Ma, please help me brush today," said Ria, unable to forget her dream. She was afraid to go to the bathroom alone.

After brushing her teeth, Ria asked, "Ma, I hope you have made BREAKFAST for me and I won't have to take fruits to school."

"Why are you asking this? I have made your favourite *pakoras* and *aloo paratha* for tiffin," replied Ma. Then, Ria told her about the dream. Ma laughed when she heard about the DREAM and said, "Whatever we think, we see in our dreams. There is no need to be scared. Forget about it and get ready for school."

By then, Ria had calmed down. "Ma I will tell everyone in school about my dream. They too will enjoy it a lot!" she said, going to school.

~ ❋ ~

JUST ASKING

By S Varalakshmi

Fufu the Fox lived in Sundarvan.

One of his favourite pastimes was troubling other animals.

So, naturally, the animals avoided getting into a conversation with him. Those who were unaware of his behaviour suffered the brunt of it.

One day, he decided to go to the local market. As he neared the market, he adjusted his glasses, which had slid down his nose, and looked around.

He spotted a shop selling TOFFEES and made his way there.

SHOPPING FOR TOFFEES

Bobo the Bear greeted Fufu with a warm smile since Fufu was his first customer that day.

He asked, "What would you like, Sir?"

Fufu looked at the neat display of assorted toffees in the **GLASS** jars and asked, "How many flavours do you have?"

Bobo proudly answered, "As many as 60, Sir."

Fufu asked again, "What flavours?"

Bobo rattled off, "Vanilla, **strawberry**, chocolate, mango…"

He was out of breath by the time he named the last flavour.

He said, "I assume you are buying the sweets for your kid, Sir. If I may make a suggestion, you can buy a little of everything."

Then, he asked hopefully, "Well, Sir, what flavours would you like to have? How much shall I pack for you?"

Fufu shook his head and said, "Hmm, sorry, but I don't want anything."

Bobo was shocked and cried out, "But why?"

Fufu smiled and replied, "Oh, firstly I was just curious to know what flavours you had. That's all. Secondly, I don't have a kid, and thirdly, I don't eat toffees!"

Having said that, he happily left the shop, leaving Bobo tearing his hair out in **frustration**.

ON TO THE POT SHOP

Next, Fufu went to Jinnie the Giraffe's pot shop. Fufu stood there for a minute and inspected the pots.

Then, he asked after pointing to one, "How much for this pot?"

Jinnie replied, "₹100, Sir."

Fufu asked in disbelief, "₹100? That is way too much! You are asking for the MOON."

Jinnie thought for a moment and replied, "I will give it to you for ₹90 then."

Fufu shook his head and said, "No, no. It is still too much."

After bargaining for a while, Jinnie said firmly, "I will give it to you for ₹75. That is my last offer."

Fufu nodded and said, "Okay. *THANK YOU*."

Saying this, Fufu turned to leave the shop.

Jinnie called after him, "Sir, aren't you going to buy the pot?"

Fufu shook his head and said with a smile, "No."

Jinnie asked in annoyance, "Why not?"

Fufu replied, "Oh, I just wanted to know how *CHEAP* I could get it for, that's all."

This annoyed Jinnie very much, but she couldn't say anything and was left fuming.

ELLIE TAKES REVENGE

Ellie the Elephant, who owned a chocolate shop opposite Jinnie's saw this.

Noticing the chocolates, Fufu remembered his wife asking him to buy a large chocolate bar from the market so that she could make **CAKES**. And he knew she would get very angry if he forgot to buy it!

So Fufu hurriedly went to Ellie's and asked, "That's a fine-looking chocolate bar. Exactly the kind I am looking for. How much does it cost?"

Ellie asked in response, "How much are you prepared to give?"

Fufu thought for a while and said, "Well, ₹400."

Ellie smirked and replied, "What? Just ₹400. That is way too little, Sir," and shook her head.

Fufu was **FURIOUS** with Ellie for not accepting his offer.

He had half a mind to walk away, but the thought of his wife's anger, if he returned empty-handed, made him feel scared. So, he increased his offer.

He reluctantly said, "Okay. I will pay you ₹800."

But Ellie REFUSED the offer once again. Helpless, Fufu kept bargaining with Ellie and finally said, "I will pay no more than ₹2000 because that is all I have. So, it is settled at ₹2000. Here is the money. Give me the chocolate bar."

But, surprisingly, Ellie didn't take the money

Instead, she said firmly, "I am not selling this chocolate bar."

Fufu was stupified. He cried out, "Not selling the chocolate bar! What do you mean? Why did you keep bargaining with me then?"

Ellie smiled and replied calmly, "I just wanted to know the maximum price this chocolate bar would fetch me, that's all."

Fufu was dumbfounded—he had been OUTWITTED at his own game for the first time in his life.

Needless to say, after this lesson, he stopped troubling other animals.

~ ✺ ~

JERRY HELPS THE BOOKS

By Poonam Mehta

It was late in the night when Jerry the Giraffe heard someone **sobbing**. He immediately got up from his bed and went to the study room from where the sound was coming.

He switched on the lights. There was no one there but he could still hear the sound. When he looked closely around the room, he saw a **BOOK** lying on the table crying.

THE BOOKS TELL JERRY THEIR PROBLEMS

Jerry immediately picked up the book and wiped its tears.

"Why are you crying?" Jerry asked the encyclopaedia.

"My friends and I are upset. No one likes to **READ** from us these days. It seems we are of no value," it said between sobs.

"Kids don't even look our way," squealed a tiny storybook from the shelf.

"That's not true. You have been around for centuries. Whatever progress man has made has been recorded within your pages. Not only do you spread knowledge but you also **entertain** kids," Jerry comforted them.

"But of late, we are being replaced by computers, smartphones, tablets and gaming consoles. Children think we are boring," said another book.

"They look at us with **DISGUST**. Children don't like to read from us. They think we are a burden," said a subject book.

Some comic books that were listening to the conversation joined in. "We have interesting stories and artwork. And yet children don't want to read us too," they cried.

"Even we feel neglected. Children use the internet to find meanings for words," said the dictionaries sadly. All the other books had something to complain about too. They were all unhappy.

Jerry felt bad for all of them. He remembered how books used to be given as gifts for birthdays, how they were always carried along during long journeys and how they kept children occupied during summer holidays. But that has all changed now, he thought.

Jerry asked all the books to remain CALM and promised to do something to help them.

JERRY HAS A PLAN

After a few days, Jerry invited all the kids in his neighbourhood for a get-together. That evening, they all turned up at Jerry's house excited about the yummy food they were going to get. But they were surprised when Jerry announced, "We will eat CHOCOLATES and cakes after each of you finish reading just one chapter of a book that I give you!"

The kids first protested but they realised that it would be simpler to pretend to read and then eat all the food. So they agreed. Each child was handed over a STORYBOOK— Katy the Kitten was given *Puss in Boots*, Betty the Frog got *The Frog Prince*, Abby the Mouse was lent *The Town Mouse and the Country Mouse*, Tina the Tiger cub was handed *The Jungle Book* and Benji the Fox was given *Fantastic Mr. Fox*.

Though, at first, the kids merely pretended to read, soon, the stories began to interest them. One chapter became two, then three and so on. The kids were completely engrossed in the books and lost track of **TIME**. They had even forgotten to ask for a refill of the snacks. When they were all done reading, they went up to Jerry to thank him.

"The stories were great! We didn't realise reading books could be so much fun. We want to read some more. Would you have some for us to take home?" they asked eagerly.

"Of course. You can take any book you want from here. And once you are done, you can return it and take another one— just like a library," said Jerry.

All the kids went home with a new book, much to the delight of their parents.

JERRY RECEIVES AN AWARD FOR HIS WORK

During an event organised in the FOREST, Mayor Rio the Rhino, announced a special award, to commend his hard work.

"I am happy to honour Jerry with an award for his efforts in promoting reading among the kids of the forest," said Rio.

Jerry was taken by surprise. He was extremely happy. After collecting the award, he immediately went home.

"Thank you," he said to the books. "I have received this award because of you." All the books were HAPPY to hear it. They were sought after once again. And Jerry never heard the books cry again!

SCIENCE IN THE KITCHEN

By Siddhesh Bhusane

On her way back home from school, all Divya could think about was the **SCIENCE** project she had been assigned that day. As she entered her house, she remembered that her neighbour, Rekha, loved science. "She may be able to help me with my project," thought Divya.

After changing her uniform, Divya went next door to meet Rekha, who was watering plants in her kitchen **GARDEN**.

EXPLORING EVERYDAY SCIENCE

"Hello, Divya! Back from school? What brings you here?" asked Rekha.

"*Didi*, we have been asked to work on a science project at school for which I need your help. Our subject is 'Kitchen Sciences' and I am clueless as to how **KITCHEN** and science could be related," said Divya.

"Hmm," said Rekha, smiling at Divya. "It's confusing but if

you observe closely, you will notice that a kitchen is as good as a science LABORATORY."

"Really? Like a chemistry lab?" asked Divya puzzled.

"Ha! Not exactly like a chemistry lab, but there are several applications used in a kitchen. For example, when your Mom makes curd out of milk, what she is actually doing is introducing bacteria, called lactobacillus, into the milk that cause the curdling of milk," explained Rekha.

Divya listened in awe, while Rekha continued to explain. "Also, take the example of pickles. When pickles are made with raw mangoes or LEMONS, lots of salt is added to them. The salt acts as a preservative that prevents the pickle from going stale. Similarly, to store wheat and rice grains for a

long period of time, we add *neem* leaves to the container. *Neem* leaves act as a natural PESTICIDE by keeping insects away from the grains."

Alum

"These are interesting facts, *didi*!" said Divya, enthusiastically writing them down. "Can you please give me more examples?"

"Sure! Once, when I cut myself and the wound began to bleed, my Grandpa told me to apply turmeric powder to the wound to stop the bleeding. Turmeric has antiseptic and antibacterial properties, which makes it effective in killing harmful bacteria and prevents the wound from getting infected," said Rekha.

Another fact that you might find interesting is that the CAKE🎂—that you love so much—is the result of chemistry. When you put the cake batter in the oven, the heat causes the ingredients like flour, butter and baking soda to react with each other and result in the finished fluffy product. The baking powder and baking soda release carbon dioxide, which adds bubbles to the batter and helps it EXPAND."

"Wow, *didi*! My classmates are going to be amazed to learn this," said Divya excitedly.

REKHA'S KITCHEN-BASED PROJECT

"These are only a few examples, Divya. There are so many more applications of science in the kitchen. But with these few examples, you may be able to put your project together," said Rekha.

"Of course! Thank you, *didi*. I now understand the use of science in the kitchen," said Divya happily.

A few days later, at school, Divya demonstrated and explained the various examples that Rekha *didi* had mentioned for her science project. Everyone loved her project and Divya received first prize for it. She thought, "Thanks to Rekha *didi*, I got first **PRIZE**."

~ ☀ ~

COMPLETE THE PICTURE

PUZZLE TIME

Parts of this image have been left blank. Look at the picture, complete it and then colour it.

THE HOMEWORK DILEMMA

By Dr K Rani

When Dino the Donkey came home from school, his mother said, "Son, wash your hands quickly and have your lunch. Then, you can watch TV."

Dino put his bag aside, washed his hands and went to the dining table. He asked, "Ma, is this lunch or dinner?"

"A meal in the afternoon is called **LUNCH**, and one at night is called **dinner**."

"But the food on the table is the same as what we ate last night. So, this must be dinner too!" said Dino.

His mother burst into laughter and said, "Son, lunch or dinner is determined by the time of the day the meal is eaten, not by what we are eating. There was leftover food from yesterday's PARTY. So, I heated it for you."

"Okay, I understand," said Dino and enjoyed the food.

A HARD-WORKING STUDENT

Dino was simple and innocent. He took things literally. Because of this, his classmates at school often made fun of him. But Dino did not take anything to heart and laughed it off.

Beri the Deer was his best friend. She understood him well.

Dino was also good in his **studies**. He worked hard and never failed in any class. Everyone at home knew this. He never lied. If he ever made a mistake, he would admit it and tell the truth.

His class teacher was pleased with him. She knew that his classmates bothered him, so she often had to explain to the others, "We should respect all students in the class and shouldn't harass anyone unnecessarily."

Though most of his classmates listened, there were a few students who did not stop harassing Dino.

Beri helped Dino in his studies. If Dino did not understand a lesson taught in class, she explained it to him in simple words.

Their teacher gave them homework every day. Most of the students finished their homework on time. Dino also did his homework regularly. If he needed help, Beri came to his rescue.

DINO GOES ON A HOLIDAY

One day, Dino's dad planned a trip to a nearby hill STATION over the weekend as he didn't have to go to the office. He booked a HOTEL for two nights.

Dino was excited about the trip. After coming back from school, he set his bag aside, quickly had his meal and got ready. Then he set off happily with his parents.

Dino did not even realise how the two days went by, as he was enjoying himself so much. He spent the holiday enjoying good food, going on scenic walks and sightseeing from morning till evening.

They returned home on Monday morning. His mother prepared breakfast and said, "Quickly get ready for school, Dino!"

WHAT SHOULD DINO DO?

Then, Dino remembered that he had not completed his homework. He said, "Ma, I won't go to school today. The teacher will scold me. I haven't completed my homework."

"It's okay, Dino. You can ask her to excuse you. But if you miss school today, you'll miss all the lessons too."

"Please, Ma!"

"Son, we returned home early this MORNING so that you could go to school. Now, you have to," his mother said.

Dino picked up his bag and left for school with a sad face.

Beri saw him and asked, "What happened? Why do you look so upset?"

"I couldn't finish my HOMEWORK," and he explained everything to Beri.

"You must have had a lot of fun at the hill station."

"Yes, I really enjoyed myself though I missed you. Ma and Dad made a sudden plan, and I did not have any time to tell you about it."

"No problem. We'll go together some other time. But you'll get scolded by all the teachers today."

"It doesn't matter. Let's see what happens," said Dino.

DINO RESOLVES THE SITUATION

The school bell rang, and after the morning assembly, the classes began.

The first period was science. The teacher arrived and said, "Good morning! I gave you homework on the last day we met. I hope everyone has completed it."

"Yes, Ma'am," said the children in unison, except for Dino, who sat silently with a sad face.

"What's wrong, Dino? Why are you so quiet? Have you done your homework? Tell me."

"No, Ma'am, I couldn't do it."

"Yesterday was a **HOLIDAY**. And still, you couldn't do your homework?"

"Ma'am, I went on a trip with my parents."

"So what? You should have carried your notebook with you.

You would have had plenty of time at night to complete the homework," she said.

"No, Ma'am, I couldn't have done it there."

"Why not?"

"Ma'am, you gave us homework. But we were staying at a hotel. It wasn't home. How could I do it there?"

All the children burst into **laughter**. Even the teacher could not control her laughter. She asked Dino to sit down and said, "Yes, you're right! But homework doesn't have to be done at home. It can be completed anywhere away from school."

"Yes, Ma'am! I'll keep that in mind for the next time. I thought homework must be done at home," Dino said.

The teacher was still laughing at Dino's response.

She **NARRATED** the story to the other teachers in the staff room. They laughed out loudly, too.

None of them asked Dino about his homework that day. By telling the truth, he saved himself from being scolded.

~ ~

THE STRANGE DINOSAUR

By Satish Roy

Jingo the Giraffe lived in Anandavan forest.

He was known to be sly and **CUNNING**. He had a habit of taking loans from friends and constantly staying in debt.

Whenever anyone would ask him to return the money he had borrowed, he would give them the same answer each time, "I am not going to run anywhere with your money. I will return it to you sometime later."

Gradually, everyone in the forest realised his true nature and started refusing to lend him any money.

JINGO HATCHES A PLAN TO GET MONEY

One day, Jingo visited Monty the Monkey and said, "Monty, I need a loan of ₹2000 from you. I will return it soon."

"Jingo, I can't lend you any more money. You have already **borrowed** a large sum of money from me. You have to return that amount first," replied Monty.

Disappointed, Jingo walked away. He asked other animals to lend him money, but all in $vain$.

He started pondering, "Everyone knows that I am in debt. I need to think of some new tricks to borrow money from them."

A few hours later, Jingo went to Anandavan Bank. He met the bank manager, Bholu the Bear, and said, "I am looking forward to starting a new **BUSINESS**. I need to borrow an amount of ₹2 lakh from your bank."

"Alright. Take this **APPLICATION** form. Fill out the details and submit them along with all the required documents. Within a week, the loan will be credited to your account. Each month, you'll have to pay the instalment money along with the interest amount to clear the loan," explained Bholu.

Jingo filled out the form and submitted the required documents along with it. Soon, the loan amount was credited to his account.

A month later, an employee from the bank visited his house to collect the first instalment, only to find the door locked.

Upon inquiry, the bank discovered that Jingo had already left the forest and ESCAPED.

The bank filed a robbery case against Jingo at the police station.

Time passed by, but there was no news about Jingo.

TERROR IS UNLEASHED IN ANANDAVAN

Then, one day, early in the morning, the forest was bustling with turmoil.

The animals of Anandavan were running hither-tither. Everyone had expressions of fear on their faces.

Monty saw Rani the Squirrel and asked, "Rani, what is going on? Where are these animals running away to?"

"Monty, a mysterious creature has been seen entering Anandavan. And everyone is running to take a look at this creature," Rani answered in a gasping voice.

Monty walked there too, and it was crowded with animals.

Amidst the crowds of animals, a strange creature could be seen standing. It looked like a giant-sized lizard. This creature was making movements, sometimes with its large mouth, and sometimes with its long curvy tail.

"W..W..Who are you? W..W..Why are you here in this forest?" Monty asked the creature quivering with fear.

"I am a dinosaur. My name is Cacto. From today onwards, I am going to live in this forest. All you animals will have to serve me. Anyone who opposes me or refuses to obey my orders will have to bear the consequence of death," roared Cacto.

At this, Dingo the Elephant said, "But dinosaurs already disappeared from earth billions of years ago..."

"Yes. At the time dinosaurs were going EXTINCT from the earth, I went inside a cave and hid. I kept myself safe by living there. After billions of years, when I stepped out again, I came here. I am now the only dinosaur on this planet," Cacto growled. The animals felt scared.

Dodo the Donkey started pleading, "We will do as you say. Kindly tell us what we need to do."

"If you wish to stay alive, each animal living in Anandavan must make a ₹500 tax deposit to me each day. I have a big appetite too. Each day, I must receive sufficient fresh, delicious food. This area will become my home. If anyone fails to abide by my conditions, you all will bear **MISERABLE** consequences," Cacto warned.

CACTO HARASSES THE ANIMALS

From the following day, all the animals followed Cacto's orders. Cacto kept a large box in the middle of the ground and each day, all the animals deposited **money**  in it.

Cacto would rest and relax all day long. When he felt hungry, he would demand meals from the animals and almost immediately, large quantities of **DELICIOUS** food would be presented to him.

Days passed like this. One day, Cacto announced, "From now on, your tax deposit will be double. All animals will pay me ₹1000 each!"

THE ANIMALS DECIDE TO DO SOMETHING

Hearing this new **DECLARATION** from Cacto, the animals of Anandavan were worried and decided to have a meeting to discuss the matter.

Monty spoke, "Cacto's demands are increasing daily. In order to deposit money to keep ourselves safe from him, we're having trouble managing our households with a limited budget. To feed him, we have to starve ourselves."

Agreeing with him, Dingo said, "You're right. We must get rid of this Cacto."

Rani said, "But Cacto is much more **POWERFUL** than us. We can't do anything to make him move."

"I have an idea," and Dodo explained his strategy to the animals.

Then, it was time to put their plan into action.

Dingo and Monty went to Cacto and said, "Cacto, you are a **guest** in our forest. We don't think you should stay outside in this hot weather. We have found a cave for you. It has all the facilities like electricity, a fan and a lot more. We have

decided that from today onwards, that cave will be your new home."

Cacto was delighted. He said, "Even I have been looking for a place to live. This ground is certainly too hot."

And so, Cacto walked together with Dingo and Monty towards the cave.

When they reached, Monty said to Cacto, "Let's go inside the cave."

On entering the cave, Cacto screamed, "It's so dark here. There is no electricity or fan either. I feel suffocated inside. You told me that all those facilities would be inside the cave."

"Do not worry at all. Everything has been arranged for you. Just wait a while. Let me turn on the light for you," Dingo echoed.

Walking quietly, Monty and Dingo secretly SLIPPED out of the cave.

At the cave's entrance, the other animals had already gathered. Together, they blocked the entrance by rolling a large rock. Cacto was trapped inside the cave.

Cacto yelled, "Why have you all trapped me in this place? Get me out of this cave. I am not able to breathe."

THE TRUTH IS REVEALED

"Cruel dinosaur! This was our strategy to teach you a lesson. You are reaping what you sowed. You lived inside a cave for billions of years. Now go back into a cave and spend the rest of your life inside it!" Monty shouted.

Cacto started begging for help. "I lied to you. I am not a dinosaur. I am Jingo the Giraffe. I have never lived inside a cave before. Please get me out of here!"

The animals were astonished to hear the truth about Cacto. They removed the rock from the cave's entrance.

Jingo stepped out. He was carrying a dinosaur mask in his

hands.

"You have been fooling us by wearing this dinosaur mask!" Dodo shrieked.

"Yes, after taking the loan from the bank, I left the forest and escaped into the city. Seeing this dinosaur mask DANGLING outside a shop there, I thought of the idea of becoming a dinosaur. I already knew it is quite easy to fool the innocent animals of Anandavan. I planned to extract a big sum of money from all of you so I could take it away and settle in the CITY. But today, I got trapped!" Jingo said sadly.

"Jingo, you have betrayed us. You have broken our **trust**," Dingo grumbled with rage.

"Jingo, there was already a police case filed against you for **robbery**. You won't be in this cave now. You can spend the rest of your life in a police station instead," Dodo said, grinding his teeth.

The animals thanked Dodo for his brilliant strategy.

Everyone was relieved to get their money back!

~ ~

COMPLETE THE PICTURE

PUZZLE TIME

Jingo the Giraffe is hanging out with his friends.
Parts of this image have been left blank. Look at the picture,
complete it and then colour it.

MAYA AND THE TIME MACHINE

By Dipannita Ghosh Biswas

Little Maya was eagerly waiting for her next school vacation to begin. Every morning, she would walk up to the **calendar**, strike a day out and count the remaining days on her tiny little fingers. She would then pack her school bag, push in the tiffin box, say goodbye to her pet dog, Boss, and rush to the bus stand to wait for the school bus.

Even though she eagerly looked forward to the summer holidays, Maya loved going to school and meeting her friends each day. She enjoyed new things—a book maybe or a board game or a toy. The latest thing she was infatuated with was a time machine. She was reading about it in the storybook she had borrowed from the school library. Once, in class, she was **daydreaming** about what life with a time machine would be like and was caught by her Maths teacher—Ms Latha. The result was that Maya was asked to write the tables of 10 to 15 a dozen times.

MAYA IS GIVEN AN IMPORTANT TASK

When she got home, Maya played with Boss for a while before she sat down to complete her homework. Uncle Gurunath had come over and was talking to her parents about his latest invention. Maya would usually have a leisurely **dinner** with her family but today she gobbled her noodles down and dashed to her room. Though Maya loved to listen to Uncle Gurunath's stories, she had to finish reading the book from the school library because it was due to be returned the next day and she didn't want to leave the story incomplete.

She sat on her bed when Boss entered the room, jumped up on the bed and curled up near her feet—his favourite bedtime position.

She opened the **HARDBOUND BOOK** in her hand…almost 40 pages left and just half an hour before Mom came to shut the lights out.

Maya kept reading as Boss snuggled closer…Suddenly, Uncle Gurunath and Maya's parents came into the room. "I have an important mission for you," Uncle said. "My time machine was declared the invention of the century and, hence, I want to keep it away from anyone with mean intentions. I have hidden it in this house and I need you to guard the room when I am not working on the machine. Your parents have agreed that you can help me with this." Maya wanted to read her book but she agreed—partly because she was curious but more so because she was awestruck! "A real time-machine, wow!" she thought.

THINGS TAKE A STRANGE TURN

Uncle Gurunath left after dinner and Maya was on guard. As she sat near the machine, she heard a sound. Maya wanted to check where it came from and **STUMBLED** upon the wire hanging loose from the machine. Her elbow hit the knob, a bright spark followed—so bright that Maya was blinded for a moment.

She looked around and saw she was in the same room—a sense of relief followed. She went out of the room to check if her parents had been disturbed by the sound, that's when she saw that two camels were standing in her front yard, **munching** lazily on dried grass. Where did they come from? Maya looked around again to make sure she was still at home. Everything seemed familiar, except the camels. She started feeling anxious.

A few minutes passed by before Maya decided to tiptoe out of the house cautiously.

She looked left and right but saw nobody. She walked up to one of the camels. Little Maya stood tiny against the camels **looming** large in front of her. Her mother had shown her pictures of these animals in some books and Maya had once seen them on the TV too. As she was about to turn around to go in search of her parents, one of the camels stooped down. There was a rope ladder hanging off its back, invitingly. Maya didn't think twice— she clambered atop the camel. As if on cue, the majestic animal stood straight up.

A TRIP BACK IN TIME

Maya held on to the sides of the jute sack that served as a seat on the camel's back. She had no idea where the camel was headed to. She was hoping that the **CAMEL** would take her to Uncle Gurunath so they could sort this out. All she saw was unlimited sand—just like the sand she had seen on her last holiday to Pondicherry. The only difference from then and now was that she couldn't spot the sea yet. The camel walked slowly. Maya looked here and there, hoping to figure out where she was.

Soon, she sensed some activity ahead. Maya strained her eyes and saw some men pulling huge blocks of stone while other men were on **HORSEBACK** riding beside them. They were busy with a construction—something very big and grand. The camel continued walking towards the structure. She saw that the men were dressed in short, pleated skirts, like the ones she wore on her school's PT days.

Maya was now close enough to the main area where all the action was. She strained her ears to catch bits and pieces of conversation floating in the air. One word caught her attention—PYRAMID. She looked around again, aghast. She was standing in front of what seemed like a pyramid under construction. Now, how was that possible? Maya kept staring at the men toiling hard under the sun, hoping to catch a glimpse of Uncle Gurunath—he had to be here! But alas, all the faces were unfamiliar. The camel suddenly came to a halt and Maya was shaken out of her reverie.

BACK HOME

Thud! "Ouch, that hurt," said Maya. She felt a splash of water on her face and tried to blink her eyes open. It was dark. Then, she heard a yelp. She sat up, eyes wide open. Boss was licking her face frantically. Maya looked around. Her bright pink floral-printed BEDSHEET was the first thing she spotted. The clock read 6.00 a.m. She stood up and her eyes fell on the storybook.

No, Maya couldn't complete the remaining 40 pages of the book but she did travel through the time machine to an unknown land—the land of history, riches and mysteries. She had gone to Egypt, home to the MAGNIFICENT pyramids. Maya rubbed her eyes and headed straight for the calendar hanging on the wall…with glee she could see that there was only one day left for her vacation to begin!

~ ~

THE MYSTERIOUS SOUND

Vivek Chakravarty

It was a cold winter night and all the animals of Champakvan were fast ASLEEP when suddenly, the entire forest trembled with a frightening, mysterious sound.

The animals leapt out of their houses and gathered in the open ground.

A MYSTERIOUS NOISE

"Where is that **frightening** sound coming from?" asked Jumbo the Elephant, yawning.

"Who knows? I know just as much about it as you do," snapped Blacky the Bear, angry at being woken up in the **MIDDLE** of the night.

"Is it possible that all of us are making too much **FUSS** about the noise?" asked Meeku the Mouse. His comment angered everyone.

"Meeku, if only a few animals had heard the sound, it would not have been **SCARY**, but all of us hearing it means there must something about this sound that we need to find out," explained Cheeku the Rabbit.

"You do have a point," Meeku nodded.

All the animals were discussing the **SOURCE** of the mysterious sound when they heard another scream.

"Who was that? First, the sound and now someone is screaming? Something is definitely wrong in the forest," said Blacky, his voice stuttering.

"Could it be a ghost?" said Damru the Donkey, shivering with fear.

"Ghost! Where's the ghost?" asked Jumbo, startled. Damru's

question had woken him out of his slumber.

"We don't know! We just heard a scream," answered Blacky.

"*Aah*! I want to go back home," cried Jumbo.

"Wait, Jumbo. I can still hear someone. It seems **someone** is crying out for help, but I can't see him. It must be a ghost," said Damru.

"Of course, you cannot see me. I am crushed under Jumbo's heavy trunk!"

"Under my trunk?" said Jumbo and lifted his trunk. He was

surprised to see Meeku crushed under it.

"Jumbo, you might as well have just killed me today," Meeku moaned in pain.

"I am sorry, Meeku! I was so sleepy that I did not realise when my trunk fell on you," APOLOGISED Jumbo, his face red with embarrassment.

"Everyone, please stop DISCUSSING these small matters and let's focus our attention on investigating the source of the sound," said Cheeku.

"Who knows? We can't even hear it now," said Blacky, suddenly not bothered about the sound.

"Wait a minute! All of us are gathered here except for Jumpy the Monkey. Is it possible that something has happened to him?" asked Cheeku.

"Oh yes! Jumpy isn't here. Could he be in some trou—?" before Jumbo could finish his sentence, he saw Jumpy striding towards them.

"What was that frightening sound?" asked Jumpy.

"All of us are trying to discover the same thing. Jumpy, where were you? Why did it take you so long to come here?" asked Cheeku.

"When I first heard the loud, *SHRILL* sound I was so frightened that I thought it would be best not to step out of my house. Therefore, it took me so long to come here," Jumpy whispered slowly.

"Alright. Let us end this discussion now. The sound is no longer **AUDIBLE**, so let's all return to our homes and sleep peacefully," said Cheeku.

Everyone agreed.

CHEEKU INVESTIGATES

Everything in the forest continued as usual for a few days, but then, again, one night, that frightening mysterious sound was heard.

The animals again gathered and tried to find the source of the sound, but couldn't. The noise continued on some nights and more and more animals started feeling scared by the mysterious sound.

Soon, animals of Champakvan stopped stepping out of their homes at **NIGHT**.

Cheeku was disturbed by the behaviour of all the animals. He could not understand why the animals were so frightened by a sound that was not harming them. He tried **EXPLAINING** this to the animals, but no one listened to him.

He decided to solve the mystery of the frightening sound.

From that day, Cheeku stayed up at night and roamed around the forest to find the source of the frightening sound.

A week later, just when Cheeku had stepped out of his house at night, he heard the same scary sound. He quickly ran in the direction of the sound, and to his surprise, he landed up at Jumpy's house.

Suddenly, the scary sound stopped, and it became dark inside Jumpy's house. Someone had switched off the lights.

"That's strange! The lights were on when I came here and the sound could be heard. But as soon as the sound stopped, the lights went off. Should I go inside and check if Jumpy is alright?" thought Cheeku.

He was just about to ring the doorbell when he heard Jumpy's voice, "I can't even practice because of this sound!"

Hearing him, Cheeku rang the **DOORBELL**. "Who's there?" Jumpy asked.

"It is me, Cheeku! Please open the door. I know that the frightening sound is coming from your house." Hearing this, Jumpy immediately opened the door.

THE CULPRIT IS FOUND

"Cheeku, please don't tell anyone else that the scary sound comes from me practising my **MUSICAL** instrument," pleaded Jumpy.

"Jumpy, I am unable to understand why you have been frightening everyone in the forest by playing such loud sounds at night?" asked Cheeku angrily.

"I didn't mean to frighten anyone, Cheeku. On the first night, when I started practising my musical instrument, one of the wires of my headphones that are connected to the instrument, was ripped and this caused that shrill scary sound that frightened all the animals. But I couldn't gather the **COURAGE** to tell everyone that it was my fault."

"I was certain that if I fixed the headphone wires, they would not make that sound again. But I wasn't able to fix them properly, and so now and then, when I practised, the damaged wires would make that **LOUD**, frightening sound," Jumpy explained.

"But why didn't you inform the animals about this after a few days?" asked Cheeku.

"How could I? The situation had blown up so much that I was scared if I told the truth to anyone, all the animals would beat me up. I haven't been able to **PRACTISE** during the day, because the animals would know that I am the source of that frightening sound."

"Jumpy, that sound created such terror in everyone's minds. They are afraid to step out of their house at night even if there is

an emergency. If you tell them the truth, they may get upset initially, but I am certain they will all **forgive** you, and you will then be able to practice peacefully," explained Cheeku.

"Also, you should purchase a new set of headphones so that they stop making this frightening sound," added Cheeku.

"Oh! Why didn't I think of that earlier?" muttered Jumpy scratching his head.

"Do you promise to inform the animals about the mystery of the scary sound now?" Cheeku asked.

"But Cheeku, if I purchase a new set of headphones, do I still need to explain to the animals about the mysterious sound?" asked Jumpy not wanting to own up.

"What if the new set of headphones gets damaged too?" asked Cheeku.

Understanding that it was **important** to explain, Jumpy nodded his head and went out to apologise to everyone.

WHERE ARE THE NUMBERS?

By Alka Aggarwal

"Raghav, wake up!" Raghav's mother called out to him, drawing the curtains open.

"Mummy! Why did you wake me up so early?" asked Raghav, rubbing his eyes.

"It's not early. It's almost 8.30," said his mother.

Raghav looked at the clock and was SURPRISED. There were no numbers on it.

A STRANGE OCCURRENCE

"Mummy! Why are all the numbers missing from the clock?" asked Raghav.

"Haha! I think you are still dreaming, Raghav. Now, go and freshen up," said his mother.

After brushing his teeth, Raghav went to the living room. There, he saw his father searching in the cabinet for something.

"What are you looking for?" Raghav asked his father.

"I am looking for a cheque that I had kept inside the drawer last evening. I have to deposit it at the bank today. But I can't seem to find it," said his father. Raghav's father found the CHEQUE under a book. To his shock, the cheque only had a signature and the bank's name on it. All the numbers, like the cheque number, account number and amount, were missing.

"This is strange. There are no numbers on this cheque.

I am sure it wasn't like this when I put it in the drawer yesterday," said Raghav's father puzzled.

Just then, Raghav's grandmother came out of her room and said, "All the dates in my calendar are missing!"

Raghav looked at his father's phone and noticed that the numbers on the phone were missing as well.

Raghav rushed to his friend Rehaan's house next door to check. All the numbers in their house were missing, too—from the remote, calendar, newspaper and even the currency notes!

Soon, the entire city was buzzing with the news of the missing numbers. Everyone was BAFFLED.

THE NUMBERS ARE UPSET

Little did they know that the numbers were actually on **STRIKE** and had returned to their own kingdom Numberland to complain to their king.

"We don't want to go back, Sir. We are being mistreated

and overused by the humans," said Zero.

"Zero is right, Sir. A student's high marks are CELEBRATED but low marks are frowned upon. Similarly, the numbers in their wallets and bank accounts are given undue importance. The lives of the humans revolve around us. From report cards, banks and phones, to addresses and clocks, the humans use us everywhere!" complained Eight.

Five said, "You worry about not being valued while I worry that a lot of kids and even adults being scared of us. Do we look like monsters? We don't mean any harm."

"Dear friends, I understand your concerns and they are valid. But you must realise that we play an important ROLE in the human world," said the king. "The humans use us to organise their world and give fixed value to things, like the price of an object, temperature, distance and time. Without us, the world would be in chaos, like it is now, since you have left," explained the king.

"If that's the case, why are some of them scared of us?" asked Five.

HUMANS AND NUMBERS LIVE HARMONIOUSLY

"That is because they are yet to fully understand how to use us. We shouldn't feel bad about that. Instead, we should be PATIENT for them to learn. So many humans love us," said the king.

The numbers finally understood their role in the human world. They thanked their king for making them realise it.

When the numbers returned, the humans were RELIEVED. Everything was now back to normal.

In their absence, not only had the humans realised the importance of numbers but also how they had been stressing on numbers more than human values.

That night, Raghav looked at the numbers on his clock and said, "Thank you for coming back, friends, and for showing us that numbers and values should go side by side. We had forgotten that **lesson**."

~ 🌟 ~

MAZE

Raghav and his friends are on the lookout for numbers. Help them find their way through the maze to reach the other side.

12345

* Answer on the last page.

THE GHOST IN THE WELL

By Omprakash Kshatriya

Shaina was on her way home from her aunt's house when she passed an old, ruined well. She heard a strange noise and looked around, not knowing where it was coming from.

The sound seemed to be coming from the well. She looked inside but couldn't see anything, although loud noises were coming from it.

Shaina called out, "Who's there?"

SHAINA HEARS MYSTERIOUS SOUNDS FROM THE WELL

Her voice **echoed** through the well. She then remembered people telling her about the GHOST in the well. Scared for her safety, she quickly ran away.

The more she ran, the more she could feel someone following her. The sound seemed to be coming closer. She quickened her **PACE**. Suddenly, she hit something and fell.

"Oh, no! Now, I'll be dead!" she shrieked.

The person following her caught hold of her and shook her vigorously, asking, "What happened, Shaina?"

"W... W... What?" Shaina stuttered and looked up.

It was Aunt Naina standing in front of her. Shaina breathed a SIGH of relief and told Naina Aunty everything—the noises, the well, and the sound following her.

"Come then. Let's see the ghost," said Naina Aunty. She held Naina's hands and began walking towards the well.

THEY SEARCH FOR THE GHOST

Shaina was scared but Aunt Naina was with her, so she gathered the **courage** and went toward the well.

"Aunty, is there a ghost in the well?" she asked curiously.

"Yes, there seems to be" Aunt Naina smiled, "I am trying to find it."

Hearing this, Shaina asked, "Aunty, aren't you scared of the ghost?"

Aunt Naina looked deep into the WELL trying to locate the ghost.

"If it was out here in the open, I might have been scared too. Since it is inside the well, I'm not scared. Why be scared of something we cannot see?" Aunt Naina said.

Aunt Naina dialled the Forest Department's number. Before ending the call, she said, "Please make arrangements to bring it out safely, or it might die a painful death inside the well."

Hearing this, Shaina asked, "Do ghosts die too?"

"Yes," said Naina Aunt, "Anything that is born has to die one day. That is the law of nature."

Soon, officers from the Forest Department arrived. One officer stepped out and asked Aunt Naina, "Is it in this well?"

"Seems to be," she answered.

AN ATTEMPT TO GET THE GHOST OUT

The officer signalled to his worker. They arranged for a huge cage to be put inside the well. The cage had some food and water to drink.

Shaina couldn't understand what was going on. What was the CAGE for? Before she could ask Aunt Naina again, the officer asked, "How did it get into the well?"

Aunt Naina knew the entire story, but she narrated a short version of it.

"Due to the shortage of forests, he might have WANDERED towards the city in search of food or water. Maybe he was thirsty and came near the well to drink some water. That is when my oxen saw him and made a NOISE."

"Alright," the officer said, "What happened next?"

"One of the oxen is brave. It ran towards him, and he ran away. To save himself from the oxen, he climbed atop the well's railing. Due to the railing being ruined, he might have fallen inside."

"Alright. We'll get him out." Saying this, the officer said something to his workers, and they lowered the cage in the well.

Shaina and Aunt Naina were GAZING into the well and they heard some movement inside.

Something black was moving towards the cage. As soon as it came close to the food in the CAGE, the cage door was shut.

The officers waited for some time. That black thing was hungry and thirsty; it began eating quietly. Shaina still couldn't understand what the thing was.

After some time, the **WORKERS** started pulling the cage.

Seeing the black ghost in it, Shaina was scared. It was frightening. As soon as the cage was pulled out, Shaina, who lived in the city, and had never seen this thing before, asked, "Aunty, what is this black ghost-like thing?"

AUNT NAINA EXPLAINS WHAT THE 'GHOST' REALLY IS

"Don't you know what it is?" Aunt Naina asked. "This black ghost is a bear. It lives in the **jungle**."

Shaina had never seen a **bear** in her life before. She was embarrassed for some time before she and Aunt Naina started laughing loudly.

Shaina said, "Oh! We are always **SCARED** of unknown things and call them ghosts."

"Yes," Aunt Naina said.

Once the officers had left, they started walking back home.

The Forest Department team had taken the bear away to get it **treated** before it would be set free in its natural habitat.

~ ~

GENIE AND JOHN

By Megha Kadam

John was a very lazy boy. He was not interested in going to school or studying regularly. His parents and teachers were always scolding him for his **laziness**.

John's parents tried to teach him the importance of hard work, but he did not listen to them.

"John, I don't know when you will realise that being lazy is not good," said dad.

"Why do you tell me the same thing every time? I wish that there was someone to study on my behalf and take exams for me," thought John.

JOHN'S WISH COMES TRUE

One morning, John went to the beach for a walk. He was dreaming about a life where he did not work and was still happy.

While walking on the **BEACH**, John hit something hard on the ground. It rolled a little ahead and made a sound that grabbed John's attention.

John was surprised to see a **GOLDEN LAMP** decorated with a small, delicate design. He thought, "This lamp looks like the one from Aladdin's story. In the story, when the lamp is rubbed thrice, a Genie appears to fulfil our wishes. Let me try."

John was very excited and he rubbed the lamp thrice.

Poof! A **Genie** appeared in front of John. He couldn't believe his eyes.

"Hello, master. I am here to fulfil your wishes," said the Genie in a pleasant voice.

John was very excited. He first asked for **chocolates** and **icecreams**. Within a few seconds, they appeared in front of John. He asked for some more wishes which the Genie fulfilled instantly.

"What is your last wish, my master?" asked the Genie.

John thought for some time and said, "I want the maths **question paper** set by our teacher for our exam."

"Your wish is my command, my master! But don't you think it is wrong to cheat in exams?" asked the Genie, concerned.

"This is my order to you, Genie. Do not try and preach to me," said John, angrily.

"As you say, my **MASTER**!" said the Genie and disappeared in the air. John was very happy about getting the paper.

BE CAREFUL OF WHAT YOU WISH FOR

"This time I will score full marks. Hard work is not necessary," said John. He practised a few questions from the paper and made chits for others.

"I will copy the answers during the exam," said John before going out to play.

John's maths teacher, Mr Thomas had set the paper on his computer. One day before the exam, he wanted to take printouts of the paper. But when he searched for the file on his computer, he found that the paper was missing.

"Oh no! Now I will have to set a new question paper," thought Mr Thomas.

The next day, John was full of CONFIDENCE when he entered the examination hall.

John snatched the paper in a hurry to fill the answer sheet. But soon, he realised that none of the questions matched the question paper that the Genie had given to him. John felt angry and cheated.

That evening, John rubbed the lamp to call the Genie again.

THERE ARE NO SHORTCUTS TO SUCCESS

"You are a cheater, Genie! You gave me the wrong question paper. I'm going to FAIL because of you," shouted John, angrily.

The Genie explained, "When you asked me for the question paper, I took it from your teacher's computer. But the file could only be in one place at a time. When I gave the paper to you, it was deleted from your teacher's computer. He set another paper after that."

John realised his mistake. He understood we have to do our work ourselves with sincerity.

"Had I studied seriously, I wouldn't have to look for a shortcut to succeed in this exam. I should have listened to my parents," thought John.

John turned to the Genie and said, "Thanks for your help. I just want you to be there to show me the right path in the future."

The Genie happily said, "My master, your wish is my command!"

~ ☀ ~

SANYA'S STRANGE ENCOUNTER

By Dr K Rani

It was a Saturday. Sanya was waiting for her father to come back from the office. The clock struck six, and, finally, her father came home.

As soon as he entered, Sanya demanded, "Dad, do you remember you promised to take me to the BEACH for a stroll today?"

"I do remember, but I am very tired today," her father replied.

"Please! I have been waiting for you for so long. I have been looking forward to this day all week," Sanya insisted.

"But it is already dark outside," her father tried to explain.

"It does not matter, Dad. We can have fun even in the DARK," Sanya continued.

Finally, her father agreed, and they walked to the beach. Sanya was aware that her father was tired, so she said, "Dad, I want to jog along the sand. You sit here and rest while I jog."

"But Sanya, I won't be able to relax, as I will be worried about you," her father replied.

"I will not go very far, and you will be able to see me," she said.

SANYA MEETS A STRANGE CREATURE

He agreed. After a few minutes, Sanya noticed a huge shining object falling into the sea. She could not understand what had happened.

Then, she saw something walking toward the beach in a sky-blue COSTUME. It was coming towards Sanya.

Sanya looked at it carefully and could not understand what

it was. She was not afraid, but as it came closer, it looked a little **STRANGE**. It was covered from head to toe in its sky-blue costume.

It was wearing some kind of glasses and holding a matchbox-sized object in its hand.

Sanya asked, "Who are you? And where are you from?"

It blinked as Sanya asked these **questions** but did not respond.

"Can you not hear me?" Sanya asked, but there was no reply. The object in its hand was moving in all directions. The moment the object turned towards Sanya, she asked, "Is this a camera to take pictures? Why are you taking my picture?"

When she did not get any response, Sanya stepped closer and stretched her hand to touch the creature.

Sanya felt an **electric** shock and pulled her hand back immediately.

It then dawned on her that this creature was an **alien**  and she thought, "What if he is from some other planet and has come here for research?"

As soon as she had this thought, Sanya blurted out, "It seems like you are an alien. I will go and tell my father about you right now."

The moment Sanya turned around, she heard a **high-pitched** sound. It was so loud, it almost made her unconscious.

She saw the strange being walking back towards the sea as she lay there.

The pitch was so high that she felt like she had gone deaf for a few minutes afterwards. She lay there and watched the creature go back.

Minutes later, the shiny object that had fallen into the water flew back into the sky. Sanya noticed that it was built like a car and had a small light at the top.

As she gained full consciousness, Sanya walked back to her father. On seeing her, he asked, "What kept you for so long?"

SANYA TELLS DAD ABOUT THE ENCOUNTER

"Dad, I saw an extraordinary creature here at the beach," and she narrated the entire incident to him.

Her father started to **LAUGH** as he heard Sanya's story and said, "I told you not to watch those nonsensical TV serials. It is because of those serials that you are now seeing aliens here at the beach."

"No, when I tried to touch it, I felt an electric current," Sanya argued.

"Okay, let it be. If you are done with your **stroll**, can we go back home now?" her father asked.

"Sure," she responded and they walked back home.

Later, Sanya's father told his wife to monitor Sanya's TV watching habits.

"Roma, now she has even started to daydream. Please ensure that she doesn't watch TV for long. It has started to affect her intelligence," he said.

"Why? What happened?" Roma asked.

Sanya's father told her mother about Sanya's story regarding her 'encounter' with an extraordinary creature on the beach.

Sanya, however, was not ready to accept that the incident was a creation of her mind.

She was **CONVINCED** it was true. She continued to think about it and could not concentrate on anything else.

The next day was a Sunday, and Sanya got up late. Her father was watching the news.

"Good morning," she wished her father. "How are you this MORNING?" he asked.

"I am fine," she replied.

DAD LEARNS THE TRUTH

Suddenly, there was news on the TV, "Last evening, an Unidentified Flying Object (UFO) was seen in the close VICINITY of our town. It left our planet before any information could be collected."

Sanya's father looked at her and said, "You were probably right, Sanya. Apparently, there was a sighting of a UFO that landed on the beach last evening."

"Dad, it had an alien too," Sanya said excitedly.

"Okay, but keep that to yourself. No one is going to believe you, and they will only question your story, just like me," her father suggested.

"Dad, it all happened so fast that even I could not believe that it was an alien. They just took a few PHOTOS and left immediately. They even took a picture of me. I hope they will not cause any harm, Dad," Sanya said with concern.

"No, do not worry at all. Nothing will happen to you here. Just relax. Yes, you might become a HERO and be popular on their planet, though," her father laughed.

"I don't understand," Sanya said, confused.

"The same way we see pictures of strange objects in our newspapers, that alien might use the **communication** medium on their planet to show your picture to the other beings there," explained her father.

"You are right, Dad. I am sure they will!" laughed Sanya.

Her father started to laugh too.

The thought of being **FAMOUS** on some other planet made Sanya feel thrilled about the whole event.

~ ☀ ~

MAZE

Help Alto Asteroid reach home.

* Answer on the last page.

THE ALIEN VISIT

By Mallika Sukumara

Rihanna lived in a plush mansion with a landscaped garden. She went for her evening walk in the garden with her dog, Darby, who loved sniffing around, as dogs do.

Suddenly, Darby darted off and went over to a peepal tree. Rihanna followed him and saw something shining under the tree. It was a huge multi-coloured stone.

She picked it up and inspected it. Her father was a **jeweller**, so Rihanna was aware of many precious stones. She thought, "I have never seen this kind of stone. I will show this to Dad."

After her father, Omkar, came back from his office, Rihanna said, "Dad, I found this stone in the garden."

Her mother, Aruna, also returned from **office** and saw the stone. She said, "It's so beautiful!"

Omkar and Aruna looked at the stone carefully. Omkar said, "It looks like a rare gem."

Aruna asked, "Where did you find it exactly? Show us tomorrow morning."

Rihanna said, "Okay," and Darby barked, "Woof, woof!"

THE FAMILY MEETS ALIENS

The next day, they went to the place where the gem was found. Darby had scampered to the spot beforehand. Rihanna said, "It was right here yesterday, underneath this peepal tree."

Omkar looked carefully at the surroundings to find some more clues about the gemstone's origins. Aruna looked above, in the branches of the peepal tree.

She pointed up and said, "I see something quite big GLEAMING amongst the branches there."

Omkar and Rihanna gasped. The 'thing' between the branches fell. Rihanna yelled, "An alien!"

The alien had glowing blue eyes that looked like sapphires and a mouth as red as a ruby. Only it did not have a nose or ears.

It had two hands and two legs, just like humans, and its whole body was rock-like, with gleaming, multi-coloured gemstones, which looked like a mix of glittering blue, yellow, red, green and orange with splashes of pearl-white thrown in.

Everyone was taken aback. Rihanna looked at the small gemstone in her hand and the alien in front of her. She exclaimed, "It's the same! This gem matches its body."

The alien stood silently. Suddenly, a small, oblong spaceship soared down from the skies and landed softly in their garden. Darby went, "Woof, woof, woof!"

Rihanna said, "Be quiet, Darby. Let's unravel the mystery of this gemstone and the spaceship. I feel as though we are in a science **FICTION** movie."

Rihanna was a fan of science and particularly space. They all waited with bated breath to see what would unfold.

The spaceship door opened. A figure similar to the one from the tree walked towards them.

Rihanna and her parents froze. A wide-eyed Darby felt safe being with Rihanna.

GETTING TO KNOW FEMI AND NOVA

The second alien joined them. It said, "I am Femi from the planet Gemelli. We were carrying gemstones from planet Earth and since this was my friend's first trip to Earth, he opened the door of the **SPACECRAFT** by mistake and fell on the tree in your garden. That's his ring in your hand."

The first alien said, "Yes.

I am Nova—and, yes, that is my ring in your hand. Our bodies and even our **accessories** are made from the most precious gemstones found on Earth. We need them to make our future generations."

A shocked Rihanna said, "Aliens! Never heard of your planet! You take gemstones from our planet to make your future generations!"

Omkar asked, "Why? Why do you need them from our Earth?"

Alien Femi said, "We need gemstones to make our bodies. We are not made of flesh and blood like you. Your planet is very rich in minerals and gemstones. There are many hidden gems here."

Aruna said, "How shocking! What if our Earth's resources dwindle because you take away its gemstones? And come to think of it, how can you speak English?"

Alien Nova responded, "We are into making many artificial things like robots and artificial intelligence. Making artificial gemstones is easy too, we just swap the artificial ones for real ones."

Alien Femi said, "We can speak any language on Earth. Our

gemstone brains are extremely intelligent! Our brains are manufactured with special **electronic** chips that understand and reply to any language or theory."

Rihanna and her parents were shocked. Darby barked, "Woof, woof, woof!"

Rihanna was angry. She said, "Artificial gemstones can never replace the originals. How long have you been taking away our planet's gemstones?"

Alien Femi said, "It has been five years since we found out about the gemstones here with our highly advanced instruments and **satellite** images using computers."

An astonished Rihanna said, "You have computers too!"

Omkar asked, "Which gemstones are you talking about? We have ammolite, opal, ruby, pearl, emerald, sapphire, onyx, topaz, diamond, and so many more." The aliens laughed.

Alien Nova said, "All those, yes, and one that's very special, indeed. It is multi-coloured and has the shine of a diamond with the colours of green emerald, yellow sapphire, red ruby, white pearl, blue topaz all mixed in it. You Earth folks have been foolish not to chance upon it yet. We have taken away tonnes of it."

Omkar and the others were shocked. Aruna said, "Are you talking about this gemstone in Rihanna's hand?"

Alien Femi said, "Yes. Our bodies are made of it."

Rihanna said, "Please find some other source or planet for making your future **GENERATIONS**. Our Earth's resources will be depleted if you don't. It's a request."

REACHING A COMPROMISE

The aliens thought about it for a while but they were a friendly race. Alien Nova said, "Only if you promise never to tell your scientists about us. Our planet is very far away from Earth, in a different **GALAXY**."

Rihanna said, "Okay. Please tell us where this gemstone is found."

Alien Femi showed them the place on the **MAP**, somewhere in the mountain ranges of the Western Ghats in India. Rihanna thanked the aliens for the information.

Rihanna gave the multi-coloured gemstone ring to Alien Nova.

Both the aliens then boarded their spaceship and said, "You Earth folk are nice. We shall miss you."

Later, Rihanna called the Archaeological Survey of India and informed them about the gemstone. Soon, the archaeologists started their investigation into the matter.

After searching for some months, they found the source of this precious, sparkling, multi-coloured gemstone, deep inside the Western Ghats.

It was all over the newspapers. The headlines were, "More expensive than a **diamond** ." Another said, "The Kohinoor among gems," and so on.

The new gem was named Indiom since it had been found in India first.

Rihanna and her family were happy and they kept the alien visit a **SECRET**.

~ ✼ ~

IGNORANCE Vs SCIENCE

By Harbans Singh

Zibby the Zebra had retired from America's National Aeronautical Space Agency (NASA) and decided to move to Champakvan forest.

Unfortunately, Champakvan, where he now lived, did not know about outer  or even about scientific facts, in general, and that was the beginning of his misfortune.

Zibby was a space scientist; he sat with his **TELESCOPE** and stared at the sky for hours, studying the **GALAXY**.

The forest animals found this habit very strange and thought he was **ODD**.

ZIBBY'S ARRIVAL STIRS UP CHAMPAKVAN

Blacky the Bear, Jumpy the Monkey, Baddy the Wolf and Jojo the Jackal had formed a notorious gang. They made money by fooling the innocent animals of the forest in the name of astrology and medicine. Zibby's arrival was not good news for their business.

Blacky was the leader of the gang. If any animal was sick, he would tell them, "You should wear a ring with a green stone and donate green gram," and then take a lot of money for his advice.

Blacky would ask animals to wear different coloured **RINGS** and donate **PULSES** of different colours, when they told him they were unwell and wanted to be healed. He even sold amulets to the animals in the name of possible 'cures' and fooled them.

"You must chant this **MANTRA** before wearing the amulets: 'I have no knowledge, I know all,'" said Blacky to Gigi the Giraffe who was sick.

"But this means that I am a fool, and I know everything," said Gigi, not convinced.

When Blacky scolded her, Gigi stopped arguing and promised she would say the *mantra* he had asked her to.

Zibby happened to be passing by and heard the **conversation**. "Gigi, this is not the right way to cure your illness. You need to see a doctor," he told her. "Come with me and I'll help you set up an appointment with my friend Dr Giro in Anandvan."

THE GANG PLANS TO ATTACK ZIBBY

The gang realised Zibby would put a **halt** to their business. At their weekly meeting, Jumpy said, "If we could prove that Zibby is mentally ill and send him to a hospital, then we would have no threat to our **ORGANISATION**." Everyone in the gang liked the idea and agreed to do it.

One day, Jumpy called all the animals of the forest together and said loudly, "What is Zibby looking for through his **pipes** all the time? And even if he finds something, how is he going to get it here? He is mad and needs to be taken to a mental hospital immediately for his own good."

Since the animals of Champakvan had never seen someone studying outer space before, they thought that Zibby was mad and everyone agreed to take him to a hospital for his well-being.

Zibby was shocked at this and explained, "I am not mad or sick; I am a scientist!"

"If you are not sick, then how come you are black and white? Why haven't you got any colour on you?" mocked Baddy.

"ZEBRAS cannot change the colours given to them by nature," Zibby argued.

"If a chameleon can change its colour, why can't you? And you claim to be a scientist! You have gone mad," Jojo said, looking at the others who nodded in agreement.

123

Candy the Chameleon was sitting on a **STONE** watching the events unfold. The noise frightened her, and her colour changed in front of everyone present.

"Can you change colour? I am not mad!" Zibby shouted loudly.

"Every lunatic thinks that. See how you are shouting!" said Jojo and everyone agreed again.

"My friends, please, listen to me! If I tell you that I am mad, will you let me go?" **pleaded** Zibby.

"When you, yourself, are admitting that you are mad then who is going to argue?" replied Blacky. Others nodded again.

"That means whatever I say—that I am mad or not—you will not let me go! Italy's famous scientist Galileo kept saying that the sun does not revolve around the Earth and that the Earth revolves around the sun instead, but people thought he was mad. They even punished him. However, today we all believe his **tHEORY**." Zibby tried to make everyone understand.

"Do you all hear what this lunatic is saying? He is trying to **JUSTIFY** himself! Send him to a mental hospital; otherwise, he is going to drive us all insane," Jojo countered.

The king of liars, Blacky said, "Friends, Zibby claims to be a scientist and says that he can blow the sun out like a candle.

That is definitely not possible. I think he needs to be sent to the mental hospital immediately."

ZIBBY IS CORNERED

Without any proof, everyone accepted that Zibby was mad. "He is mad, totally mad! And he is also a crook!" hundreds of voices shouted together. Zibby looked HELPLESSLY at the crowd.

His neighbours—the deer family, and the python with black stripes on his yellow skin, who lived on the tree in front of his house—were all looking at him with anger and BETRAYAL.

Zibby was tied up with heavy iron chains around his neck.

He felt helpless but no one in the forest stood up for him.

His face grew sad, his hope broke, his legs TREMBLED and he fell face-down on the ground.

His nose and mouth were filled with mud, which made him

cough endlessly.

The heavy chains injured his neck. A stone flew towards him from the crowd, hurting his wounds. He groaned with pain.

THINGS ARE SET RIGHT

Just then, King Shersingh the Lion arrived with four guest elephants, who had been sent by the United Nations Children's Fund (UNICEF) and the United Nations Educational, Scientific and Cultural Organization (UNESCO) to look into the forest's WELFARE.

These two organisations work for the BETTERMENT of children and create awareness about education.

After discovering the situation, they said, "Zibby is not mad. In fact, he is the most INTELLIGENT one here, and you are the fools for declaring him a lunatic. Release him immediately! He is the former professor of Space Science from NASA."

The elephants then turned to King Shersingh and said, "It is a pity that your forest does not have even one school. We will arrange for funds so that you can open a school here."

The king was delighted to hear this, as he had wanted to start a school in the forest for some time.

He was convinced that thoughts should not be based on beliefs, but on and science.

Blacky, Jumpy, Baddy and Jojo's faces fell. They tried to slip away but were caught.

Zibby was appointed the forest's education minister. Blacky and his gang members were sent to jail where they studied science and other subjects. When they were released they gave up using astrology and cheating people.

~ ⁂ ~

SEQUENCE

Like Zibby, Gina is also good at science and is making a lava lamp.
Put the steps in order and discover the magic of science.

Lava Lamp

* Answer on the last page.

A MAGICAL TRAP

By Abha Verma

Simon, the elephant-eared Squirrel, Anya, the lion-toothed Ant, and Gigi, the giraffe-necked Cat, were very close friends. All three had *magic* wands.

Once, the three of them had a competition to see which one could perform the best spell.

THE THREE FRIENDS SHOW OFF

Simon, moving his big ears, waved his magic WAND and said, "Magic wand, do your very best! Turn this little flower into a forest!"

And then the little flower became a big forest!

Anya, of course, wanted to do something as well. She started dancing while waving her magic wand and sang, "Magic wand, you are ten out of ten! Turn this grain of sugar into a MOUNTAIN!"

And then the grain of sugar became a mountain!

Gigi, of course, wanted to do something as well. She swayed her long tall neck, and said, "Magic wand, you're not just a twig, turn this little mouse into a lion, do a gig!"

And then the little mouse became a lion amid the huge forest on top of a high mountain.

The three friends were very pleased with their magic and started clapping and **DANCING** Each of them used their magic just to make the other two feel **WEAK**.

THE LION CHASES THEM

They soon started arguing with each other and were about to get into a fight when the lion roared loudly. He jumped down from the high mountain. Within minutes, he crossed the **forest** and ran to eat the three friends.

Simon wrapped his ears together like two hands and ran to save his life. Anya folded her teeth inside her mouth and hid in Simon's shaggy tail.

Where could Gigi hide her long neck? She wrapped her neck around her body and became round, like a ball, and rolled along the ground.

Gigi rolled and went faster than Simon, who ran behind her with his ears wrapped together.

The lion ran behind all of them with his mouth open, ready to eat them up!

Thankfully, the three friends were still carrying their magic wands. Simon had held it in his mouth; Anya had hidden hers in Simon's tail, and Gigi had stuck hers between her neck and legs.

As the lion approached, Gigi rolled faster, and Simon jumped and ran faster. Anya, hiding in Simon's tail, TREMBLED so much in fear that it felt like an earthquake in the forest.

THE SPELLS ARE UNDONE

Then, Simon remembered that he had his magic wand. Taking it in his hand, he cried, "Magic wand, it's time to do things slower. Turn the forest back into a flower!"

In an instant, the spell was broken. The huge forest disappeared, and the tiny flower blossomed as before.

Seeing this, Anya became **courageous**. She swung her wand from Simon's shaggy tail and cried out loud, "Magic wand, make smaller, not bigger. Turn the mountain back into sugar!"

And the high mountain **VANISHED** .

But the lion showed no sign of stopping. Soon, he was about to catch them with his wide-open mouth. Just then, Gigi realised what she needed to do. As she ran, she screamed, "Magic wand, you're not in vain. Make the lion a mouse again!"

Now, what happened to the lion? Instead of a lion, there was just a small mouse. Seeing Gigi and Simon in front of it, the mouse trembled with fear and ran away with all its might.

The three friends pulled themselves together.

They pledged to use their magic only in ways that they could handle and would **benefit** everyone, not cause harm.

~ ※ ~

MONTY AND ROBO

By Isha Agarwal

Monty the Monkey was utterly delighted. His uncle, Jacky, had sent him a **GIFT** from America.

MONTY MEETS ROBO

"Papa, let's open this box quickly!" Seeing Monty's **desperation**, his parents chuckled.

As they opened the box, Monty grew excited! "Wow! It's a robot!"

He started playing with it and exploring its **VARIOUS** features. "How do we switch it on? How does this work?"

Monty's father, Danny, pulled him aside as he was *FIDDLING* with the robot and said, "Wait, Monty! Read the instruction manual. We first need to charge this robot. So, before you start playing with it, let's charge it."

"Where is the charging point?" Danny wondered. "Hmm!

Got it!" He plugged in the robot and kept it aside to charge.

"Monty, this robot will take time to charge. Till then, why don't you call and thank your uncle?" Monty's mother, Dimpi asked.

Monty nodded and called Uncle Jacky. He thanked him for sending a cool robot and his uncle responded with delight.

Once the robot was charged, Monty's father switched it on and blue and green lights started to glow on the robot.

"Hello, my name is Robo. What is your name?" A MECHANICAL voice came from the robot.

"My name is Monty. Will you be my friend?" Monty asked, excited that the robot could talk. He was as CURIOUS as he was amused.

"Hello, Monty. Robo will become your friend."

Having heard this programmed reply from the robot, Monty jumped with excitement.

A CHANGE IN MONTY'S LIFESTYLE

Robo could do many things. It would play with Monty and help him do his homework. It could also help Dimpi by **COOKING** food and cleaning the house. Recently, it had also repaired Danny's old car. Its actions were dependent on the instructions given.

In a way, Monty had found a new friend. And this was the kind of friend Monty didn't get into fights with either.

After he started playing with Robo regularly, Monty stopped going out and playing with his real-life friends, like Bobo the Rabbit and Teenu the Elephant.

Whenever he didn't feel like studying, he would get Robo to complete his homework by **DICTATING** what had to be written. When he wanted something, he would simply sit back and order Robo to bring it to him. Slowly, Monty became **DEPENDENT** on Robo for every little thing. He turned lazy and never thought about anything except eating and sleeping and, soon, he became unhealthy.

135

His parents were worried about him. They often tried to explain to Monty that he should not get Robo to do everything for him, but Monty didn't pay any ATTENTION to their advice.

Soon enough, he put on too much weight and was unable to concentrate on his studies. In school, too, his teachers noticed this and warned him, but he ignored their words.

He had started believing that Robo was his true friend, and everyone else was JEALOUS of him because they didn't have a robot.

THE RESULTS OF MONTY'S INACTION

Soon, his school's mid-term EXAMINATIONS began. His parents' fear came true. Monty didn't score well. In addition to getting scolded by his teachers and parents, Monty was DISAPPOINTED in himself. He used to be one of the top scorers in class.

He realised that this was the result of getting most of his homework done by Robo and not doing it himself. However, the effect of this **REALISATION** lasted only for a few days. He had become so lazy that he wasn't able to do any of his tasks.

A few weeks later, his school organised the Annual Sports Day. Monty played with Robo and didn't practice for any of the events.

The Sports Day finally arrived. All the students and parents were in school. Monty had also brought Robo with him. Everyone looked at his robot with much **astonishment** and curiosity. Monty felt proud. He was more excited about displaying his robot to other students than **participating** in the Sports Day.

MONTY AT SPORTS DAY

When it was time for Monty's class to race, all his classmates **performed** well, except for him. He wasn't able to run properly during

the race.

Somehow, with much difficulty, he crossed the finish line, landing in the last position. By then, he was also out of breath. He walked towards the sidelines and stood quietly. His friend Teenu won the race.

The long jump competition was to follow the race.

When it was Monty's turn to do the long jump, he fell flat on his face with a thud. The **onlookers** burst into laughter. Upset at what had just happened, Monty started crying.

His friends stepped forward and lent their support by stopping the onlookers from making fun of him. Within a few moments, Monty's parents and his teacher, Mona the Bear, also came up to him.

"See, Monty. Previously, you were so active. You were among

the top-most participants of our Sports Day. And today, you are not even able to complete a race. This is the result of getting too dependent on your robot," Dimpi said, expressing her concern.

"Besides that, Monty, look at all these friends of yours. Remember how you discarded them and behaved badly with them after getting the robot? And today, they stepped forward to support you," Danny added.

MONTY REALISES HIS MISTAKE

Monty lowered his head in embarrassment. "I am sorry, Mummy and Papa! From now onwards, I will try to be independent."

Turning to his friends, he said, "Sorry! I have realised that you are my real friends." Bobo and Teenu stepped forward and hugged Monty.

His teacher added, "We should move forward in life by learning a lesson from this EXPERIENCE. We should not remain dependent on machines for tasks that we can do ourselves."

From that day onwards, Monty restarted his habits of physical exercise and playing with his friends.

He became fit, active and energetic. Teenu and Bobo supported him.

Like before, Monty started to perform well in his studies. Also, he started doing all his **tasks** by himself.

The robot in their house was charged only when needed, mostly to play when Monty's friends came over.

A DAY AT THE SEA

By Megha Kadam

Riya's father was a fisherman. She had never gone fishing with him. But for the past few days, she had wanted to go with her father.

"Dad, please? Can I join you today?" Riya pleaded as she saw her father leaving for work.

"Riya, I will be **distracted** if you accompany me. I won't be able to handle your mischief and concentrate on fishing."

"But Dad, I promise I will sit quietly and just watch you fishing. Please let me come, Dad!" Riya kept on asking her father.

RIYA GOES FISHING

Her father gave in, "Okay, Riya! But don't do anything **NAUGHTY** while we are on the boat!"

"I promise, Dad!" said Riya feeling thrilled.

Riya was happy to see the huge **SEA** while travelling across it on the boat. She was surrounded by water as far as she could see.

Her dad and the other fishermen started to spread their nets to start fishing. She kept on watching them. She was curious to see how fish were caught in the nets. Riya was also hoping that a huge whale would get caught in her father's net.

After a short time, she got bored, as she couldn't see any fish being caught. She began playing with the water while bending over a little from the **BOAT**.

The waves touching her hands made a mesmerising sound as she moved her fingers in the water.

Suddenly, she felt a soft-textured thing touching her hands. Riya was surprised to see a tiny golden-red **FISH** cheerfully tapping against her hand.

The little fish was trying to play with Riya. As Riya realised this, she kept showering water on it.

RIYA AND DAISY PLAY TOGETHER

The fish tried to escape from the water Riya threw at it. It kept jumping up and down and was smiling at Riya with sparkling eyes. Riya was excited too.

After some time, the fish came close to Riya and said, "Hi! My name is Daisy!"

"Oh no! You can speak?" asked Riya aloud, surprised.

"Yup! I can!" giggled Daisy as she **twirled** in delight.

"I don't believe this!" Riya was still startled.

"Ha! Ha!" Daisy **GIGGLED** in her magical voice again.

"What is your name?" asked Daisy.

"My name is Riya. So, tell me Daisy, what do you do all day?"

"I like playing the whole day! My mother keeps scolding me. But I love to explore the world around me. I like chasing the boats and ships that come to the sea every day."

"That's great, Daisy! You are adventurous and also very cute! I'm so glad to have met you!" said Riya patting her.

"Thank you!" Daisy responded, giggling and twirling gleefully again.

"But I'm afraid Daisy; someone might catch you!" said Riya.

At that very moment, her dad saw her playing with the **BEAUTIFUL** fish. He shouted, "Riya, grab it quickly! It will fetch us a good amount!"

Riya was shocked at her dad's words.

"Yes! Yes, Dad!" she replied as her voice shattered.

THE FRIENDS PART WAYS

The moment her dad turned his back, Riya WHISPERED, "Daisy, please go away from here as soon as possible or else you will get caught!"

Daisy looked at Riya innocently. "Oh! But I still want to play with you," she replied.

"No, Daisy! Please listen to me, or else they will catch you."

"Okay! Will you come again to play with me?" Daisy asked.

"Yes, sure! I will come, Daisy!" said Riya with a heavy heart.

"Daisy! Daisy!" Daisy's mother was calling her. "Come soon!"

"Yes, Ma!" Daisy said and waved goodbye to Riya.

Riya heaved a sigh of relief when she saw Daisy turning away, **flapping** her fins beautifully.

Riya's dad called her out, "Did you catch that tiny beautiful fish?"

"No, Dad. I'm sorry, I couldn't!" replied Riya without looking

at him.

"Better luck next time! Anyone would pay us a lot for that beautiful fish!" he said.

Riya didn't utter a word.

She just kept PRETENDING she was sorry about not being able to catch the fish.

By then, her dad had caught a lot of fish. But Riya was not as excited now as she had been at the beginning of their trip.

Her mind was captured by Daisy. Such a beautiful, lively, attractive and cheerful creature she is! And a talking fish too! Unbelievable!

"I hope no one ever catches you, Daisy!" Riya murmured as they started their journey back home.

As she looked back, she saw Daisy taking long jumps in the sea to wave goodbye to her!

Riya's face lit up and she waved back.

Riya's father kept wondering who Riya was bidding goodbye to! But only Riya knew that secret!

~ ~

COLOUR ME

A TOUR OF OUTER SPACE

By Neelam Rakesh Chandra

"Where's Preetika? I can't see her," said Grandpa, looking for Preetika.

"She must be enjoying her HOLIDAY by sleeping in. Let me wake her up," said her mother.

She went to Preetika's room and smiled. The room was a mess, and Preetika was fast asleep.

She touched Preetika on her head *affectionately* and sat on the bed.

"Preetika! Preetika! Wake up! How long will you sleep? I know it's Sunday, but wake up now," Mummy said, shaking Preetika.

Preetika woke with a start. "Mummy... I..." she said, *rubbing* her eyes.

"What? It's time to get up now!" Mummy said, smiling.

"Mummy! I'm...I'm here...But how...?" asked Preetika.

"Where else will you be? Are you still sleeping? Get up, come on!" her mother said, amused.

"No, Mummy, listen to me," Preetika said, rubbing her eyes again.

"What is it?" Mummy asked, sitting beside her.

PREETIKA TELLS MUM ABOUT HER OUTER-SPACE ADVENTURE

"I was taking a tour of outer space!" Preetika said.

"What?" asked Mummy, surprised.

"Outer space! I was roaming in space!" replied Preetika.

"Roaming in space?"

"Yes, Mummy! Laika came last night and asked me if I wanted to visit *outer space*. I immediately agreed and set off with her," said Preetika excitedly.

"Laika? Who's that?" Mummy asked, shocked.

"Don't you know Laika? Our teacher told us yesterday that Laika was the first **DOG** to be sent to outer space by the Soviet Union in their spacecraft, Sputnik 2."

"All right, all right! Now get up!"

"But listen, Mummy!"

"Yes, tell me!" smiled Mummy. She had started enjoying Preetika's story.

"I sat on Laika's back and left for outer space. Laika is an adorable dog!"

"Okay, I'm glad to hear that. And then?"

"From above, I looked down and saw how the earth looked. Everything appeared so tiny, like tiny toy houses and little trees. When we went higher, everything became *BLURRED*, and I couldn't make out the houses anymore. The rivers were like blue lines drawn across the planet."

"Oh! And weren't you afraid of being so high up?" Mummy asked.

Preetika shook her head and said, "No, Mummy! The height

wasn't scary. But when we left the earth's atmosphere, I was **SCARED**. I was screaming out for you!"

"What? Why was my **brave** girl suddenly feel so scared?" asked Mummy affectionately.

"As soon as we left the atmosphere, I started flying!"

"You, what?" asked Mummy wide-eyed.

"Yes, I lifted off Laika's back and started floating around. I was actually **Flipping** around! I was so scared!"

"Oh, my poor daughter!" said Mummy. "What did you do then?"

"I was screaming out for you: 'Mummy! Mummy!' But Laika was quite smart. She floated closer to me. Then she asked me to fasten myself to the belt attached to her. As soon as I did that, I got to use a part of her **spacesuit** too. I was so surprised."

"Spacesuit? What's a spacesuit, Preetika?" asked her Mummy.

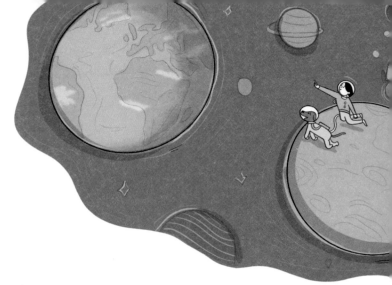

"People can't go into outer space in ordinary clothes. They have to wear a special suit known as a spacesuit. It is made of special materials. It has a system for supplying **oxygen** to the person wearing it. People can't breathe in outer space because there's no oxygen up there. Spacesuits help astronauts to breathe and move about easily in space."

"Ah, you seem to know a lot about outer space. So, tell me: why did you start floating suddenly?"

"Well, outer space lies beyond the reach of the earth's GRAVITY. So, we became weightless and started floating like light objects. It was scary at the time, Mummy, but now I find it amazing."

LIFE IN SPACE

"When I was hungry, Laika gave me something to drink.

Astronauts can't eat solid objects in outer space, so they carry food in liquid form. 𝒞𝓇𝓊𝓂𝒷𝓈 from solid foods could float around and get into the astronauts' eyes and cause trouble. So, they have to float around, stay upright and drink their food," Preetika continued.

Mummy responded, "I see."

"And there's another amazing thing!"

"What's that?"

"When I was drinking the liquid food, I spilt some of it. That became a big drop and started floating too! Laika took me to the drop, and I quickly **GOBBLED** it up!" Preetika said, laughing..

Her Mummy laughed with her too.

"Oh, and the earth looks blue from outer space," Preetika added.

"Blue?"

"Yes, Mummy! And then Laika took me to the moon as well. She showed me the footprints of the astronauts who had visited previously. Those prints are still there!"

"How's that possible, Preetika? They must have gathered dust over the years and faded away by now," her Mummy said.

"No, Mummy! The moon doesn't have any atmosphere. So, there's no wind, water, or rain, and there's no dust flying around either. Everything stays exactly as it is," Preetika explained.

"Oh, I see."

"And I forgot to tell you another thing!"

"What's that?" Mummy asked.

"Laika showed me a wall on the earth and told me it's the Great Wall of China."

"Yes, the Great Wall of China is the biggest wall in the world, and it's one of the world's Seven Wonders as well," said her Mummy.

AN EFFORT TO PRESERVE THE ENVIRONMENT

"Yes, Mummy, we could see it, but it was hazy. Laika said that in earlier years, astronauts could see it clearly. But due to the increasing pollution on earth, it appears hazy now. Laika asked me to go back to earth and request all my friends to plant one tree each and do everything we can to preserve the environment. I'll keep my promise, Mummy, and talk to them tomorrow in school," Preetika said decidedly.

"Yes, definitely! Tomorrow I'll get a sapling for you. You can plant it in the park nearby," said her Mummy.

"No, Mummy! I'll have school tomorrow. It's Sunday so I'll plant it today. Can you get me a *neem* **SAPLING**, please?"

"All right! Have your breakfast and get ready! Then we'll go to the plant nursery."

"Thanks, Mummy! I'm very happy today!"

While leaving the room, Preetika's Mummy said, "And the story of your dream gave me a tour of outer space too! Thank you!"

COLOUR ME

THE SPECIAL TREATMENT

By Dr Rajiv Gupta

Harry the Fox had a farm in which he grew different kinds of vegetables and sold them at the market. Now, it was the season for bottle gourds. Since they were in high demand, Harry sold his big, peerless bottle gourds at the market for a handsome price.

Recently, some eggplants had **SPROUTED** from the patch nearby. They were in awe of the bottle gourds.

"Oh my! How beautiful you all look!" one of the eggplants complimented the bottle gourds.

"Thank you! We are indeed beautiful," said the bottle gourds, admiring themselves.

"But how is it that some of you are unusually big?" asked another eggplant.

HOW THE BOTTLE GOURDS GREW BIG

"There is nothing **UNUSUAL** about it. Our master gives us vitamin injections every day, early in the morning. They help us grow big and healthy," said one of the bottle gourds, swinging in the air.

"Vitamin injections? Why? Are you unwell?" enquired the eggplants.

"No. Vitamin injections are given to make us more **beautiful** since master loves us the most," replied the bottle gourds proudly.

The eggplants were jealous of the special treatment that the bottle gourds were getting. They wanted to see those vitamin **INJECTIONS** and, if possible, get some for themselves. They did not like the way they looked—dark and stubby.

A MYSTERIOUS BOTTLE IS FOUND

Early the next morning, the eggplants waited eagerly to see what injection their master Harry administered to the bottle gourds. Freida the Fox was walking by when she noticed the little eggplants HUDDLED behind the leaves, their gaze focused on the bottle gourds.

"Hello! Looks like somebody's secretly ADMIRING the beautiful bottle gourds," said Freida smiling.

The eggplants were taken by SURPRISE. They did not expect to see Freida so early in the morning. She usually came to the farm later in the day to collect fresh vegetables for Dr Giro the Giraffe at whose house she worked.

"What injection does our master Harry administer to the bottle gourds that makes them grow so big and beautiful?" asked the eggplants, EMBARRASSED.

"What injections?" asked Freida curiously.

"The bottle gourds said there are some vitamin injections that Harry gives them every morning so that they grow big and strong," replied the eggplants.

Freida recalled that just the previous day she had made bottlegourd JUICE for Dr Giro and he had sent it back saying it was too bitter. And many animals had come to Dr Giro's clinic complaining of food poisoning and the common food that all of them had eaten was bottle gourd.

"I think Harry has already given the bottle gourds the injection. See! There's a bottle lying under their creepers," said an eggplant.

Freida checked the ground where the eggplant was pointing and found a small bottle. She quickly pocketed the bottle and hurried home.

DR GIRO DISCOVERS THE TRUTH

As soon as she reached home, Freida told Dr Giro about the vitamin injections that Harry was giving the bottle gourds and handed over the bottle she had found on Harry's farm.

Dr Giro ran some tests on the **RESIDUE** in the bottle. When the results came, his face turned serious.

"What is it, Sir? Is something wrong?" asked Freida worried.

"Yes, Freida. This is an **oxytocin** injection given to artificially boost the growth of vegetables. With this injection, the bottle gourds grow big and mature in just 3-4 days, so Harry is able to sell lots of them in a short span of time, and that too at a good price," said Dr Giro. "This is the reason that the animals have been falling sick after **CONSUMING** the bottle gourds."

"How does it harm our health, Sir?" asked Freida.

"Our livers could get affected if we consume vegetables or fruits with oxytocin in them for a long time. This chemical can also cause our blood pressure to shoot up, leading to diseases of the heart," explained Dr Giro.

"Oh no! Harry is causing so much harm to all the animals just for his own **greed**. We must inform the police," said Freida.

"You're right, Freida," agreed Dr Giro. He dialled the police station and informed Inspector Chetan the Cheetah about Harry.

HARRY IS APPREHENDED

The next day, Chetan caught Harry red-handed while he was injecting the bottle gourds with oxytocin. The news of Harry's arrest spread across the forest. All the animals were astonished that Harry had been injecting the vegetables on his farm with .

The bottle gourds, too, were surprised to learn about it and were ashamed of themselves. Meanwhile, the eggplants were relieved that they hadn't been injected. They no longer wished to change anything about themselves.

~ ☀ ~

ANSWERS

Page 89: Maze

12345

Page III: Maze

HOME

Page 128: Sequence